In Search Of The Maltese Falcon

written by Mario Fenech

Produced by:

FriesenPress
Suite 300 – 852 Fort Street
Victoria, BC, Canada V8W 1H8

www.friesenpress.com

Distributed to the trade by The Ingram Book Company

Chapter 1
The Finding

It was in mid July on a hot, sunny day, when the yacht *Slik* anchored a few miles out of Spain; the sea was calm and there were no clouds across the sky. The sun was extremely bright and scorching. The multimillionaire Richard Nichols, the proprietor of the *Slik*, was quietly taking pleasure looking and simply relaxing at the blue, calm water and the sunny azure sky. Richard rejoiced in sailing and he spent most of his life on his yacht, cruising around the world. Richard Nichols was forty-five years old. He at no time got married, and earned his money by gambling and venture in historic arts. His preferable pastime was to look for lost treasures. He made his enormous fortune from selling the discoveries at auctions around the world. Sailing with Richard was his right-hand man, Cyrus McCormick. Richard unfairly treated Cyrus like a servant and with no proper respect.

Cyrus worked extremely hard for his boss because he fully understood that if it was not for Richard, he would be dead, or he could have spent the rest of his entire life in jail. At the age of six, Cyrus was left unattended when he became an orphan after his mother died. After the funeral of his mother, his father took his own life because he felt that he could not live without the one he cherished. Cyrus was put in foster homes; none of the close relatives wanted to care for him because he was always getting in serious trouble. He was transferred to different foster homes. No one could cope with him; he got into lots of considerable trouble. At the age of eleven, Cyrus got into a bitter quarrel with another kid; killing the other kid during the street fight, Cyrus was arrested and jailed.

Richard does take good care of them financially; he is very short-tempered and gets angry and vicious when things do not go his way.

Cyrus decided to go for scuba diving. He takes pleasure in it, because it kept him away from Richard and helped him to relax. When Samantha saw Cyrus organizing the gear to go scuba diving, she got up and turned to Richard.

She asked, "Ricky baby, isn't it very hot up here? Why don't we go for a dive?" Samantha said while running her fingers into Richards's hair.

Richard got up and walked away, and said to Samantha, "I don't feel like it right now. You go with Cyrus," Richard replied while he walked toward his cabin. Samantha felt relief hearing that from Richard, and she took a couple steps to the railing to call Cyrus.

"Cyrus, please bring me my diving gear. I am coming diving with you."

Cyrus was astounded and did not know what to do. He ran fast up the stairs and murmured to Samantha, "Are you crazy? Do you want Richard to hit upon and we both end up dead?"

"Relax, Cyrus, I already asked him if he would like to come with us," replied Samantha.

Cyrus was relieved to hear that and asked, "Is he coming or what?"

"No, but he told me to go ahead and to go with you," Samantha replied smiling. While Samantha and Cyrus were putting on their diving gear on, Richard appealed to them, and pointed his finger at Cyrus and said, "Cyrus, you keep an eye on Sam and make sure that nothing happens to her."

"Don't worry boss, I will take care of her," replied Cyrus.

Samantha and Cyrus jumped in the blue water, and down; they went.

It was not long; Samantha suddenly saw what looked like a crate covered with seaweed and sand. She pointed to Cyrus, and they dove closer to the trunk and cleared away the sand from the top.

Samantha and Cyrus looked at each other with astonishment. What they thought it was an old wooden box turned out to be a treasure chest.

Samantha gave the finger up signal to Cyrus to surface.

When they happily reached the surface, Samantha told Cyrus, "This is it. This time we won't tell the old man."

She was very much hoping that they would keep whatever is in the treasure chest for themselves.

Cyrus, with a weak smile said, "Babe. How do you actually expect me to bring that chest up on the boat with him not seeing us? Even if we find a way, how long do you think it will take Richard to find out, then what?"

He was tempted to do as Samantha highly recommended, but he was quite certain not to take any major risks, he Samantha swims to the yacht.

Samantha was very angry at Cyrus because she knew Richard was going to be joyful about their significant finding, and she knew that Richard would not share any of the glory or wealth he would make from their big discovery. Cyrus took his gear off and asked one of the crew members where Richard was. "Downstairs in his cabin," was the reply. Cyrus headed down to Richard's cabin and knocked on the door, there was no answer.

Cyrus knocked harder the second time without knowing that Richard was sleeping.

He thumped the door for the third time. The loud angry voice of Richard called, "Who in the hell is it?"

Cyrus opened the door trying to look very happy and said, "Boss, guess what? You're not going to believe this."

"This better be good," yelled Richard, as he rolled out of bed.

"When Sam and I were diving, we unexpectedly found what looked to be a treasure chest, and I was pondering if you would like us to bring it up?"

Richard sprang out of his bed and said, "A treasure chest? Did you say a treasure chest?"

Richard shoved Cyrus out of his way as he headed to the upper deck, nearly striking Samantha down while she was on her way into her cabin.

"I hope you are completely happy," Samantha told Cyrus with a miserable look upon her face.

"Don't worry, I will find a way to keep this one for us. I will think about a good strategy," replied Cyrus.

"You have a strategy? What kind of strategy could you have? You are spineless. You didn't have the nerve to hide it from him and keep it our secret?" Samantha replied.

Cyrus put his arms around Samantha shoulders as he looked at her eyes and told her, "Trust me. You were right when you said this is it. You just have to trust me." They gently smiled and gave each other a swift kiss, and both headed up on deck.

"Cyrus, come up here, quick." Richard's loud voice could be heard from miles around. Cyrus ran up on deck. "I want you to go and bring it up," ordered Richard.

Cyrus immediately started to put back on his diving gear and told Richard. "I will require some long ropes to drag it up."

"Don't worry, we have an abundance of rope on board," replied Richard.

Richard requested one of his crew members to go down below deck and bring instantly all the rope he could find. Cyrus leapt back in the water, pulling behind him the rope to tie the chest to bring it up. As he finally reached the chest, he tried to tilt it backwards to put the rope around it. To his astonishment, when he moved the chest, it felt like it was completely empty. He wrapped the treasure chest with a net, grabbed it, and started to swim near the surface with the treasure chest in his hand. Richard was waiting impatiently on deck, as he was passing back and forth he told Samantha, "Another finding, my dear, and this time, we weren't even looking for anything."

Samantha attempted to hide her growing distaste for Richard, kissed him and said, "Yeah honey, more money and honours for you."

Richard was all smiles, but suddenly he stopped smiling. He slowly pushed Samantha away and with a displeasured look on his face, and stopped laughing; the laughter turned into anger. In front of him, there was Cyrus holding the treasure chest in one hand. "Is that it? It is that the treasure chest?" Richard softly asked with a humble voice.

Cyrus did not know what to say. As he kept holding the treasure chest in one hand he said, "Boss, I have a feeling it's totally empty." Cyrus was somewhat anxious; he was a bit fearful that Richard would think that he had stolen what was inside the chest.

Richard walked slowly towards Cyrus, went down on his knees and looked closely at the chest cover, and clutched the padlock.

It was still locked, and there was no sign that it was forced open. Richard got up, looked at Cyrus and told him, "For a minute, I thought you pulled a fast one on me."

Samantha walked slowly towards Richard, put her arms on his shoulder, and said to Richard, "It looks to me that you don't trust Cyrus? Are you trying to falsely accuse him that he will steal from you? You should be very ashamed of yourself."

Richard did not know what to say, he looked up at Cyrus and with a gentle smile said, "I am sorry, you know money can change people."

"Bring the cutting torch and let's cut this thing open," yelled Cyrus.

Cyrus cut the lock off, and everyone on deck was looking at each other querying what was inside the chest. Cyrus was not sure if he should open the lid; he remained gazing at the chest.

"Well," yelled Richard. "Are you going to stare at it, or are you going to open it?"

Cyrus arched over, took the latch off, and carefully grabbed the edge of the chest lid and slowly opened it. When the lid was fully open, Cyrus looked inside the chest; all there was were rolled-up sheets of leather. Richard quickly snatched the documents from the chest and very carefully unwound them. He noticed that on each document was a series of maps.

"What is that?" Samantha asked.

Richard looked at the maps, and you could see his eyes getting illuminated. "My dear, these are maps of a buried treasure," said Richard as he rolled up the maps back and ordered the crew to get the deck be cleaned up. Cyrus, Samantha, and Richard quickly proceeded down to Richard's cabin. Richard slowly opened the maps and laid them out on his desk. He could not make the logic of the maps, and with a bewildered look on his face, he was desperately trying to examine the maps and to determine what kind of treasure it was where it was from. Richard was an expert in treasure hunting, but he had never come across any findings like this one. In the past, he found gold and silver treasures but not maps. He was becoming totally confused and too complex to figure out the reading and the drawing of the maps. On the first map, there was a map of an island. The name "Melita" was written down across the island map. On the second map shows a main entrance that commenced to other caves. The third map was more difficult because the drawing on the map appearances a cave high above the water with the word Hassan written out across the map. He also noticed that there was a circle drawn around the image of a bird. "Melita, Hassan and the figure of a bird; what do you make out of it, Richard?" Cyrus asked.

"I don't know," replied Richard in a low discomfited voice. "It seems it is written in an Arabic language. The map of Melita and this symbol of a bird, I didn't know. This whole thing is a shamble. I don't know which one of these maps is the first or the last," shouted Richard, and he started pacing back and forth in his cabin.

"Let's look at the first map of the Island. There is a name on it, so let's look it up," said Samantha.

"Melita, I definitely never heard of such an island," replied Richard as he kept looking over the maps.

Richard had journeyed around the world, looked absolutely stunned and for once, he looked humiliated. "Melita," he said. "Where is Melita?" he kept repeating to himself.

The three of them looked displeased. For Samantha and Cyrus, because they had their personal plans for the treasure. For Richard, because he was trying to figure out where Melita was, and he just wanted to search for whatever was on the map. Richard and Cyrus looked at other maps of the world that Richard had on his yacht. Some of the maps were of his finding and were fairly old.

They carefully surveyed for hours, but found nothing acknowledging where Melita was.

Richard called the captain, and asked him if he ever heard of a country called Melita. The Captain did not know himself.

Then, unexpectedly Richard's face lit up. "Of course!" he yelled in an ear-splitting voice. "Rita would know. If anyone knew about ancient Arabic history it will be Rita." Richard called for the yacht captain and told the captain to sail back to the United States first thing early morning. The captain looked totally speechless and asked Richard what was the objective and strongly suggested to Richard that to call Rita would be simpler than voyaging half way around the world. Richard aggressively demanded that he had to go back to America.

Chapter 2
Richard's Past

As soon as the Captain left Richard's cabin, Samantha slammed the cabin door and loudly yelled, "Rita. Who in the hell is Rita?"

Richard slowly opened a bottle of rum, poured out a glass, took a sip, and looked at Samantha. "Rita," he said. "There are a few things that you don't know about me," grinned Richard.

"You're an old bastard. You've been swindling behind my back," yelled Samantha.

Cyrus told Samantha to calm down. "Sam, relax, Richard hasn't been cheating on you," Cyrus told her in a soft hearted voice. "Rita is Richard's daughter."

"His daughter?" Samantha asked in a respectful voice.

"Yes, my dear, she is my daughter," replied Richard. "And if you call me a bastard one more time, I pledge I will feed you to the sharks!" yelled Richard as he lightly slapped Samantha's face. "You don't know anything about me. I'll tell you. Sit down." Samantha poured herself a glass of rum and sat across from Richard.

"You said you were never married," Samantha said in a smooth voice.

"You don't have to be married to have children," replied Richard. "You see I was only eighteen when I deeply fell in love. My parents were extremely rich, but Rita's parents were poor and my parents would not allow me to happily marry her. She was only sixteen and we loved each other very much, first love never dies. We finally decided to run away from our families and from our town. We wanted to make sure that both of our parents would definitely ever find us.

"We stopped at a farmhouse humbly begging for food. We told the farmer that our parents died, and that we were a brother and a sister. The farmer made us a kindly offer to stay with him and his wife to work on his farm. The first night we were all alone together in the room that they gave us, and we had sex. We were fairly young and very much in love.

"We didn't know very well what to do, but real love conquers and our strong emotion took control over us. After two months, Rita fully realized that she was pregnant. The farmer got agitated when we told him the absolute truth that we were not brother and sister. The farmer's wife was very highly delightful and understanding of our situation. She somehow managed to influence her husband to let us stay with them, and they kindly took good care of us. The farmer and his wife dealt with us as if we were theirs since as they didn't have any children of their own. After nine months went by, Rita, my girlfriend, has got very sick and unhealthy, she died while giving birth to our daughter. I named my daughter after her mother, Rita."

Richard stopped to wipe the tears off, and poured himself another glass of rum. This was an awkward moment for Richard, as he did not at any time show that he had any strong emotions, which Samantha had at no time seen from him.

"I am very sorry to hear that," Samantha said. "Then what happened?" she asked.

Richard continued, "I stayed working at the farm and raised my baby with the help of the farmer's wife. About three years later, I started to gamble. Every week, I was broken, kept exhausting my wages. When the farmer found out what I was doing behind his back, he asked me to leave. Being immature and foolish I left the farm and left Rita behind.

"A few months later, one night I broke into their house and took Rita. I had to keep on looking for a proper place to stay. Finally I found a job in a stable. I took the job to keep Rita well taken care of and to have a roof over our heads. Then, one day I was given a tip on a horse race. I took a good chance, and I gambled all my savings on this horse and, luckily, the horse won the race. The horse's name was Slik. I won a fairly substantial sum of money. With all the money that I won, I no longer had to work, and I could take financial responsibility of my daughter. I sent her to the finest private schools while my luck kept constantly changing for the better. I was winning more and more money; I gave Rita the best education that she deserved. Unfortunately we don't see much of each other lately, other from time to time. Now it has been over seven years since we last come together, but I call her occasionally, and that is why I want to go back to the USA."

Rita, who did not approve of her father's lifestyle, felt that she was isolated and virtually deserted at the young age when her father sent her to the private schools. Rita lived in California, and was a professor of Science of Antiquity. She was one of the youngest respected scientists in North America, thanks to her father. Rita was a very bashful person. She didn't have any serious close relationships with any of her male friends. Although she did not well remember her mother, she always thought deeply about her. When her father used to visit her, they spent most of their time together talk over the past. Rita in her thirties was a loner; she has no family. Her father had lost completely all family contact after he ran away with Rita's mom.

Richard, Rita's father, was extremely rich, but good is the money if they do not see each other. Nearly all nights, she cried because she appeared lonely, and desired she died too when she was born.

Chapter 3
The Meeting

The subsequent morning Richard's yacht dragged out of Spain and headed towards San Francisco, California. It was a fairly prolonged journey for Richard. He was excited about his important finding, and finally, he would see his little girl after a prolonged absence.

As soon as Richard's yacht dropped to anchor in California marina, Richard directed Cyrus to call for a taxi and Richard waited impatiently. It took about half an hour for the taxi to finally arrive at the marina. At the same time, as soon as the taxi pulled in front of Richards' yacht, he ran to the taxi, opened the door, and jumped in. He gave the chauffeur Rita's address. He was only wishing that she still lived at that exact location when he last visited her. Richard kept asking the taxi driver to drive faster because he was a little impatient sitting in the taxi. The cab driver told Richard that San Francisco was a very busy city, and he wished to make sure they did not get into any serious mishaps.

Richard reclined back in the seat took a deep breath counting the minutes to arrive at Rita's house. It seemed like an eternity for Richard. Finally, the cab pulled in front of Rita's house. Richard tapped at the door, and he was panicked because he had not seen his daughter for a number of years. He rang the doorbell and a female voice could be heard saying, "I am coming."

Rita opened the door; she could not believe her eyes when she saw her father on her doorstep.

"Daddy!" she revealed with tears to her eyes as they warmly embraced each other.

"It's been a long time, my child," said Richard.

"Yes, Dad, it has been a very long time. It has been several years. Come in," Rita asked Richard; they walked indoors holding each other's hand. Rita asked her dad if he was all right. Richard at once replied by telling Rita that he is all okay.

"So what brought back after all these years?" curiously Rita asked.

Richard told Rita about the maps that he found. She anxiously asked to see the maps.

Richard pulled the maps out of his suitcase and cautiously positioned them on the table. He opened the map and asked Rita what she thought about it.

"Well, I never knew of such an island really existed. Melita seems like a rather strange name," Rita told her father as she kept investigating the maps.

"Yes, dear, that is what I said also. I looked in all my records and surveyed all of my maps but no such island existed," said Richard with dissatisfaction in his voice.

"How long are you going to stay?" Rita softly asked, expecting him to stay around a while.

"Well, I can't do anything and can't go anywhere until I find the answer to this completely mystified map," swiftly responded Richard.

Rita with a smile to her face expressed to Richard, "You can stay with me, dad, and at the same time we can try to find more about this island of Melita"

"Regrettably, I can't take you up on your offer. I will feel out of place. I am not used to sleeping in buildings, I like the fresh air of the sea," replied Richard.

"Come on, dad, the least you could do is to try to spend some time with me, unless you came here merely for my immediate assistance only," Rita told her dad as she wiped away teardrops from her eyes.

"I want to stay, but I am a bit frightened that I will do or say something that will get us to squabble. I am not the real gentleman whom I use to be," slowly replied Richard.

"Give it a try. I am sure we have a lot of catching up to do," highly recommended Rita.

"Well, if you persist, I'll stay here. Are you pleased now?" replied Richard. Rita gave her father a cuddle and a kiss. She escorted him to the bedroom where he would be sleeping. Richard asked Rita to use the phone, so he could call Cyrus. Richard told Cyrus that he would be staying at Rita's house for a while.

Cyrus delivered the very good news to Samantha, and they were happily celebrating because they knew that they would be all alone on the yacht. They could take endless pleasure in their sexual activities while Richard was temporally away. Cyrus immediately authorized the captain and the crew to take a couple of weeks of vacation.

The next early morning, Rita and Richard were carefully looking throughout some of her exploration papers, desperately trying to find where Melita was, or any other knowledge on the island. They consumed the whole week looking throughout stacks of documents that Rita possessed from her extensive researches. Unfortunately, they couldn't find anything noteworthy partly related to the island, both were getting frustrated and agitated. Rita noted that the script on the maps was originally written in Arabic, but the symbols and drawings were tracked back to the time of the Turkish pirates over five hundred years past. They could not make common sense of the three maps. It appeared that the hidden treasure was in a cave above sea level. The other map displayed that to get to the treasure; you have to go through tunnels or caves encircled with water.

Rita and Richard were very grieved because they could not come up with anything. What pestered them the most was the name of the island. They could not understand why the symbol of a bird dawning was on one of the caves.

One late afternoon, while they were doing research, Richard got increasingly irritated. He hurled all the books on the floor, started hollering that he had enough, and he was terribly tired. Rita got intimidated because she never saw Richard furious before. She told her dad to just relax, she asked her dad to go for a nice, quiet dinner. Richard expressed remorse for his behaviour. He very much agreed with Rita that they must get out of the house to relax.

"I have to call Cyrus to bring me some clean clothes before we go out for dinner," said Richard as he started to dial the phone.

Back on the yacht, completely isolated, Cyrus and Samantha were having a truly great love making time and party most of the day. They were in bed having sex when the phone rang. Cyrus politely answered the phone. It was Richard calling; he immediately notified Cyrus to bring some of Richard's clean clothing over to Rita's house. He specifically instructed Cyrus to bring Samantha with him, so he could introduce her to Rita. Apprehensively, Cyrus and Samantha hurried to take a shower, got dressed and drove to Rita's house.

About an hour later, they were knocking on Rita's door. When Richard opened the door Cyrus said, "You look like worn-out, boss. Did you have any success with your investigation?"

"No. No luck at all. We cannot find anything, nothing about that bloody damn island. Come on in. Where is Samantha?" Richard asked.

"She is in the car," replied Cyrus.

"Tell her to come in, I want her to meet Rita," replied Richard.

Cyrus went back to the car and told Samantha that Richard wanted her to go inside in order to formally meet his daughter. Samantha was not too anxious to meet Rita. Slowly, she got out of the car and looked at Cyrus as she gently smiled at him.

"Now you must properly behave," Cyrus clearly warned her, because he knew the consequences if Richard found out what the two of them had been doing while he stayed with Rita.

Samantha smacked Cyrus's ass hard, kept strolling away without saying anything. As soon as she entered the livening room, she ran towards Richard, wrapped her arms around his neck, kissed Richard on his cheek, and told him how much she missed him. Richard pulled her arms away from him and told Samantha that he would like her first to meet his daughter.

Samantha and Rita embraced. Rita could sense the cold, unpleasant approach of Samantha. Samantha spun towards Richard and asked him, "So honey, did you find out anything about those maps?"

Richard looked at Samantha and told bluntly told her that they were unable to find any useful information.

"All we found out is that these maps are over five hundred years old, but we cannot pinpoint the position of the island Melita," responded Richard.

"That's too bad. It looks like that you are going to lose this one, honey," said Samantha, mocking Richard as she looked at Cyrus.

Cyrus suddenly began to get extremely nervous, striding across the room. Suddenly, he stopped and said, "Why don't you put a classified advertisement in the newspaper?

"Put an advertisement in the newspaper?" the three of them asked almost at the same time.

"Yes. You kindly offer some money for anyone who can come up with any useful information on the location of this damn island," said Cyrus.

"Post a classified advertisement? You very well know how many weirdoes will be calling me. I will wager you that every one of them will know precisely where this island is. Then of course they will want the reward money!" yelled Richard. "Look at us, Rita and I have wisely spent nearly a whole month actively searching, and we haven't been able to find out anything. You honestly think that any jerk off the street will come and tell me where to find this damn island?" You could see the vexation in Richard's face while he was talking.

Rita got up from where she was sitting, quietly told her father to calm down and said, "Maybe it is not a bad idea after all."

"Thank you," said Cyrus.

"What are you trying to say?" Richard asked Rita.

"Dad, you put the ad in the newspaper and offer a reward for anyone who can come up with substantial knowledge about where Melita is, or where it was. You don't have to pay anyone until we confirm such facts," Rita tried to clarify to her dad.

"Do you believe that someone will give us any information without knowing why we are asking?" Richard questioned who appeared confused and annoyed.

"Listen, dad, go ahead and put the ad in the paper, and we will take it from there. We have nothing to lose," replied Rita, trying to convince her dad.

"Okay. I'll put the damn ad in the paper," Richard said as he walked towards the door. "Get off your butts, you two, we have work to do," Richard shouted aloud at Cyrus and Samantha. They got up, said good-bye to Rita and chased Richard to the car. Rita called at her dad and asked him, "What about dinner?"

"Some other time," Richard shouted back.

On her way out the door, Samantha told Rita that it was a great joy that she met her. They embraced. "Same here," replied Rita.

Richard told Cyrus to drive to the San Francisco Tribunal newspaper to place the ad. The day after, in all the newspapers in the state of California appeared a full-page ad that read: "Five thousand dollars reward for anyone who has any information regarding the island called Melita. For more particulars call this number." Richard listed Rita's phone number. A week went by, and no one called and Richard started to get very impatient. To begin with, he never stayed firmly in one place as long as he'd stayed with his daughter. He was accustomed to freely traveling and not being cooped up in one place. The ad ran in the newspaper for a week. Richard did not receive a single call. At the same time, Richard was at Rita's house waiting for someone to call about the ad, and Samantha and Cyrus were having the best time of their lives. They stayed on the yacht all by themselves and they spent most of their time having sex and, most of all, liking their liberty from Richard.

Chapter 4
The Homeless Man

It was on the tenth day after the advertisement was listed in the newspapers when, walking in a back alley, was a man in his forties with a dirty beard and wearing ripped, filthy clothes. He looked as if he had not taken a bath in months. The homeless man was looking for a quiet place to sleep for that night. He initially began to gather up some old newspapers that he found in the garbage container to use as a blanket to cover him. He set up a proper place where he wanted to sleep that cool night and in the process of covering himself, a name on one of the newspaper pages suddenly caught his notice. He picked up the page and started to read it. He swiftly got up, opened the paper, and read the article twice over. It was the ad that Richard had put in the newspaper ten days earlier. The name Melita caught his attention. He read the ad repeatedly.

Every time he read it; his smile got greater. Then suddenly, he started laughing out loud so hard that tears of pure joy rolled down his face. "Five thousand dollars! I'm going to be rich," he kept saying to himself. Hurriedly, he ran to the closest phone booth. He soon realized he had no money; he humbly begged for a quarter. The homeless man received a quarter, ran back to the phone booth, and dialed the number that Richard put in the ad.

The phone rang. "Hello," was the answer. It was Richard politely answering the call.

"Hello. I read the interesting ad in the newspaper," the homeless person said.

Richard, who had been waiting anxiously by the phone for over ten days, got absolutely thrilled. This was the first call in acknowledgement to his ad. "Yes, yes, of course," Richard quickly replied.

"You are enquiring for useful information about the island Melita? I know a lot about Melita," slowly replied the homeless man.

"Well, why don't you come over to my daughter's house, and let us see how much you very correctly know," said Richard without thoughts of who that total stranger could be.

"What is the address?" the homeless man asked.

Richard gave him Rita's address and specific directions how to get to the house.

"Okay," the homeless man replied. "I'll be there as soon as I can. It is going to take me a couple of hours to get there," he told Richard.

"That is fine; I'll be waiting, however, let me caution you: you better not be pulling my leg," threatened Richard.

"No, sir!" the homeless replied. "You want information about Melita; I have it. I have all the information for you, as long as you keep your absolute guarantee paying up the reward."

"Don't worry about the money; just be sure that you won't be dishonest." Richard hung up the phone. He called Cyrus and asked him to get to the house as quickly as possible.

Cyrus and Samantha were stripped in bed, but got dressed quickly. Uneasiness started to hit them both because Richard had never called that late at night.

"What do you think he wants?" softly, Samantha asked.

"I don't know. He sounded usual," replied Cyrus while he was putting his trousers on.

"You don't think he found out about us?" Samantha asked with a troubled look on her face.

Cyrus tried to assure her that he did not think that Richard knew about their sex affair. Although he was trying to look fairly calm, he was very worried, and he made sure that Samantha has to stay pretty calm when they got to the house. Samantha kept asking Cyrus what they would do if Richard knew about their sex life.

"I don't think he knows because, if he does, I am quite sure that we would be both dead by now. Relax," Cyrus replied, desperately trying to look totally fearless. However, deep down, inside, Cyrus was really terrified. They left the yacht and drove away to Rita's house.

They were both completely silenced, did not say a word to each other all the way to the house.

At the time, Richard received the phone call from the anonymous homeless man; Rita was at the library looking and anticipating that she could come up with some lead about the maps. Appearing at Rita's house, Cyrus parked the car and firmly told Samantha to act perfectly ordinary.

"Pretend that you missed him. Okay? Flirt with him a bit and try to make him cheerful," Cyrus instructed Samantha.

"Do I have to?" questioned Samantha.

"If you highly value your life and mine, you will," replied Cyrus, still trying to figure out why Richard called so late at night and what was the great significance to go there right away.

Cyrus rang the doorbell, Richard opened the door. Without any slight hesitation Richard told Cyrus to go and to pick Rita up from the library. Cyrus got relieved when he heard Richard telling him to go pick Rita up.

"But, boss, what is going on?" Cyrus asked nervously.

"Just do as I told you, go, and get Rita now!" ordered Richard. Without asking another question, Cyrus ran out to the car. As soon Cyrus left, Samantha felt uneasy, and she gave Richard a kiss. "Honey, it has been a long time since you and I have spent time all alone together."

Richard just pushed Samantha away. "Not now, dear; I have more important things to do."

For certain knowing that Richard called them was not about her having sex with Cyrus, she got perfectly tranquil, and she built enough courage to directly confront Richard. "That's all you care about is money, what about me? I have spent this past month sleeping all alone and just wanted you. I felt like a prisoner with Cyrus guarding me as you don't trust me," said Samantha as she poured herself a glass of rum. "Why is it so absolutely essential that you called this late and asked us to rush to get here?" She continued to agitate Richard. He totally ignored her, and he kept looking outside the window waiting for Rita to show up. Richard currently appeared to be too preoccupied to comprehend what was going on between his girl-friend and Cyrus.

It did not take Cyrus long before he was back to the house with Rita. She sprinted to the house, and soon she went in the living room she ran towards her father. "What is going on?" Rita asked him.

Richard excitedly told her about the phone call that he had received.

"Do you think he is telling the truth?" Rita asked her father, who was walking across the living room anxiously waiting for the man that had called him.

"Yes. He said that he knew a lot about Melita," he replied with a smile. "Finally, we are going to get what I have been looking for after all," Richard said as he held two fists up in the air.

Rita told Richard to sit and to calm himself. "I'm too excited to sit down," he told Rita.

At that precious moment, there was a gentle knock on the front door. "It's him! Open the door, Cyrus, and let him in," ordered Richard. Cyrus, who was sitting across from Samantha, got up and opened the door.

Chapter 5
The Information

"Mister Richard Nichols?" politely asked the homeless person when he saw Cyrus at the door.

Cyrus looked truly horrified and asked, "What do you want, beach bum?"

"I am here to speak with Mr. Nichols. I briefly spoke to him on the phone, and he gave this address. I have got valuable information about the island Melita," said the homeless man.

Cyrus started to laugh so hard that he practically fell down to the floor.

Samantha, who heard Cyrus laughing, ran towards the door and asked Cyrus what was funny. The homeless men stood still at the door, quite frightened, not exactly knowing why Cyrus was laughing at him. Cyrus told Samantha that it was the man with the useful information for Richard, Samantha suddenly also began to laugh. Cyrus told the homeless man to leave, and he slammed the door shut. The doorbell rang again, and Cyrus opened the door. There was the homeless man still standing on the doorstep. The homeless man demanded to speak to Richard. Cyrus and the homeless man got into a loud screaming argument. Richard heard all the shouting and ran toward the front door. "What the hell is going on over here?" Richard asked. "If it is him, let the man in."

Cyrus asked the homeless man to get inside and clearly warned him to keep his hands in his pockets. The homeless man intensely gazed at Cyrus and humbly stepped inside.

He did not like the way Cyrus welcomed him as he followed Cyrus into the living room where Richard was still patiently waiting. "What is this? Who in the hell are you?" Richard asked out loud with an astonished look on his face.

Cyrus was still laughing, and said to Richard, "With all the work your daughter did, and all the information you searched on the computer, nobody, and no one, not even you, boss, could come up with anything. This bum knows where that island is." Cyrus shoved aside the homeless man from the back, knocking him downward on his knees, and he went to sit down beside Rita. "This I want to hear."

"Who is Richard Nichols?" gently asked the homeless man, looking a little shaken.

"I am," Richard replied, approaching slowly towards him. "Listen, if you think this is a funny story the best thing to do is to get the hell out of here before I break your legs," said Richard in an outraged voice.

"No, no, sir! I am not joking. I do know about Melita," the homeless man replied at once. Richard walked closer to the bum, poked him in his chest so hard that the homeless man lost his composure and fell down. Everybody started to laugh, other than Rita. She quickly ran towards him, asked him if he was alright, and generously assisted him up from the floor.

She turned around and expressed in a bitter voice, "Let the man say what he has to say. At least listen to him and give him a chance."

Everyone stopped laughing, and Rita requested the homeless man to tell them what he knew. Cyrus stood up, neared the bum and said, "Let me tell you something, if it is absolutely true that you have legitimate information about Melita, then you won't have to worry; you'll be okay, but if you are fabricating it, then, bum, you are a dead man," and he returned to his seat. Rita helped the homeless man to a chair and told him to sit down. Richard gingerly approached the man and strongly reminded him that he had previously warned him about the consequences if he is untruthful.

"My name is Jason French; I read the ad in the newspaper that you are enquiring for information about an island Melita. You offered five thousand dollars reward for this information. Let me tell you, I have all the important facts you need about Melita. Don't let these tatters that I am wearing mislead you."

Jason suddenly began building some gallantry and said, "You see, five thousand dollars is a lot of money, but, for that particularly kind of information it is not enough."

"Not enough?" yelled Richard.

"No. Melita is a very old island, and now the island is called by an entirely different name. It used to be Melita over six hundred years ago," Jason replied.

"You really mean to tell me there is such an island?" asked Rita.

"Yes, there is, but the name has been altered, and that is why you could not come across any details about the island," replied Jason. "That's why five thousand dollars is not an adequate amount of money for a reward to give you any accurate information. For you people to be asking for such information about Melita, you must have found a really aged map or some kind of an old scripture. In other ways, you would never have identified the name of Melita," Jason said as he looked at Richard.

"Well, yes, that is true. We uncovered a map in Spain," gentle spoken Cyrus said. Cyrus finally began to strongly believe in Jason. Furthermore, he was also rather anxious about the island. He had his own plan for the exploration of the treasure.

"This island was under that name well over six hundred years ago, until it was changed to M..." Jason suddenly stopped talking because he quickly realized that he virtually provided them what they urgently required to know for the five thousand dollars reward.

"Changed to what?" asked Richard.

"Well, sir, that is why you have to come up with more money," replied Jason. "I know you are looking for a prehistoric treasure. Is it pure gold, perhaps? Melita was mainly occupied by many rich powerful nations and that is why this island has such a long, fascinating history. What you are looking for has to be a very luxurious historical treasure."

Jason stood up and started to walk towards the front door to leave.

"How much do you want?" Richard yelled back.

Jason opened the front door, stopped and turned around looked at Richard and said. "Two hundred thousand dollars," Jason replied without hesitation.

"Are you out of your mind?" Richard yelled, as jumped up from his chair. Jason did not want any confrontations, stepped outside, and closed the door behind him.

"Stop!" yelled Richard. "Come back inside, and we'll talk."

Jason went back inside, and strolled close to Richard and remained in front of him. Jason had the sensation that Richard would pay him whatsoever he had asked for the information, especially that Richard would not let him leave. Jason proceeded to sit on the chair alongside Rita.

Jason immediately began to speak while the others were speechless. "Without exhibition, the map that you found, describe in your own words the map, and if I can tell you what you desperately need to hear, or perhaps even the name of the island, you'll pay me five hundred thousand dollars. If you are not completely satisfied with my information, I walk out of here the same way as I came in, homeless and broke."

"Your payment went up," said Richard in a soft voice. He did not know if he should believe Jason or not.

"I have what you need, and if you want it bad enough, you will pay," replied Jason as he stood up from the chair and started to walk towards the door again.

"Wait," Richard yelled. "Let me converse with my daughter. Give us a few minutes." Richard asked Rita to go with him into the kitchen.

Cyrus pursued.

"What do you think? If we show him the maps he might give us the wrong information, and he'll go look for the treasure for himself," Richard said to Rita.

She replied, "Dad, I think we ought to give him some elements of the maps, but not everything that is written on the maps."

"Okay, but we have to be extra careful not to provide him with too much information," replied Richard.

The three of them walked back to the living room. Richard opened one of the maps and asked Jason to keep some distance between them.

"Okay, I'll stay in that corner, and you stay in the other corner," suggested Jason.

"Fair enough," replied Cyrus.

Richard progressively and anxiously carefully opened the maps. He was much undecided about the release the fine points of the maps; slowly, he began. "On one map displays a large cave. The entrance to the cave is encircled by water. On the other map is a cave high up the water level. That's all the information I can give you," Richard said. Everyone's eyes turned to Jason.

"Did you say a cave above water?" asked Jason.

"Yes," Rita replies.

Jason said, "There are lots of caves on this island and most of them are completely surrounded with water." He briefly hesitated for a brief moment. "One cave that comes to mind, and that I am fully aware of that is above the water, is Hassan's cave."

Richard got cold as ice when Jason references the word Hassan. Rita and Cyrus looked at each other yet the three of them showed no strong sentiments.

Richard looked straight at Jason and asked, "Did you say Hassan's cave?"

"Don't tell me that you people are looking for Hassan's cave?" Jason asked.

"That is the name that is written across one of the maps," said Rita.

"Do you certain know where it is?" Richard asked restlessly.

"Yes, of course. However, what are you looking for? This cave was commonly used to hide the captured individuals on the island before they were transported to Turkey and sold as slaves. There are no treasures up there," replied Jason.

"We do not comprehend what we are looking for. All we have are these maps and on one of the maps, there is what appears to be a symbol of a bird drawing next to the name Hassan," Rita explained.

"The drawing of a bird? Did you say a bird? Jason asked anxiously.

"Yes, a symbol of a bird!" replied Richard.

"The golden bird," replied Jason smiling. "Oh, people. You are looking for the most valuable priceless treasure in the world. You know how many people would like to put their hands on that treasure? So they say, this bird, was a contribution to the people of Melita and my speculation is its value is over five hundred million dollars. Treasure hunters have been looking for this bird statue for many years."

"Five hundred million dollars?"

"Let us cut the bullshit. Where is Melita? Tell me and I will write you a blank check right now." Richard reached in his pocket and pull out a blank bank check.

"I am afraid now that I know what you are looking for, the reward is up to one million dollars," Jason said with a grin on his face.

"Have you gone mad?" yelled Richard. "You don't even know if this bird statuette is still there, in the cave." Richard stood still in front of Jason with a pen and a blank check in his hand.

"Boss, I suppose this bum is definitely trying to take advantage of you. Let me throw him out of here," Cyrus said while he walked towards Jason.

Cyrus grabbed Jason by the neck and kept repeating that he was going to kill Jason.

"Let him go!" loudly screamed Rita as she started to repeatedly punch Cyrus. Richard requested Cyrus to let Jason free. "Listen, all of you. You heard him, how much this treasure is worth. What's one million dollars? Dad, think about this. After all, how did he know about Hassan's cave? Jason couldn't have said anything, and he may perhaps go looking for this stupid bird for himself," Rita yelled.

Jason lightly pushed Cyrus away from him. He was relieved when Rita backed him up besides; she just gave him an idea.

"That's right. I know where Hassan's cave is. Your daughter is absolutely correct. All I had to do is to tell you that I was sorry, and that I do not know of such a place and left. Yes, I could have looked for it for myself, but I am not that type of person." Jason walked towards Richard. "I will make you a deal, Mr. Nichols," said Jason.

"What kind of a deal did you want now?" Richard answered in a soft speech.

"You very well know I could go and look for the bird statue myself, sell it and keep all the money all to for myself, or I could sell these details to someone else," Jason replied.

"Who is going to believe you?" Cyrus asked.

"Probably no one, but are you willing to take that chance, Mr. Nichols?" Jason asked and continued, "I'll personally take you to this island and lead you to the cave. You pay me half of the reward now and the other half after the discovery of the statue. All expenses paid, of course," Jason suggested.

"One million dollars, have you gone totally insane?" Cyrus howled, as he walked towards Jason and suddenly grabbed him by this throat. Cyrus was squeezing so hard that Jason looked as if he was being choked to be dead. His face turned red, and he started to lose consciousness.

Cyrus angrily shouting at Jason and kept calling him a bum and kept repeating, "I am going to kill you, you son of a bitch. You piece of shit. You're a bum!" while he had a hold of Jason's throat.

"Stop it, stop it. Let him go!" yelled Rita while she kept constantly hitting Cyrus on his arm. Cyrus let go of Jason's throat and deliberately rammed him to the floor. Jason crouched down on the floor, supporting his neck as he tried to grasp to breath.

Rita slightly bent down beside Jason, and she asked him if he was alright. Jason, barely breathing, gestured his head that he was alright. Rita helped Jason up to his feet and assisted him to the kitchen. Cyrus followed them to the kitchen, pointed at Jason, and warned him to get out of the house, or he would kill him. Richard, absolutely stunned by what just happened, entered the kitchen and told Cyrus to leave the kitchen. Richard was not a person that is lost in words and was not concerned about anybody's well-being, looked at Rita with a bewildered look on his face.

Rita looked at Richard and told him that he had to decide what he really wants to do.

Richard approached Jason and said to him, "Hear me, son. I'll go along with your deal. I will give you the one million dollars reward. You will be closely supervised every step you make. You have to stay in this house, no phone calls. You cannot go anywhere by yourself. Wherever you go, Cyrus goes with you. One wrong move and you're a dead man. You have just seen what he could do. Do you comprehend what I am telling you?"

"Yes, sir," Jason replied in a murmured voice. "However, after this whole thing is over, the first chance that I'll have I will kill you, Cyrus." Jason pointed at Cyrus.

"I am really scared," Cyrus replied sarcastically. "However, even so, best watch it, boy, because I might kill you first sooner than you think."

"Enough you two, we are all in this together. First, we get that golden bird, and after we find that bird, then you two can kill each other, but not before then," Richard cautioned Jason and Cyrus. Richard, by this time, had returned to his normal mean personality.

"Tonight everyone sleeps in this house. Jason, you sleep down here with Cyrus. He will stay with you all night," ordered Richard.

"What about the money?" Jason asked.

"See, boss, that's all he keeps questioning. Where is the money," said Cyrus.

Richard told Cyrus to shut his big mouth and to go and get some pillows and blankets for him and Jason.

Cyrus humbly went upstairs to do what Richard asked from him.

"Tomorrow I will go to the bank and get your half of the money in cash," Richard told Jason.

"That's excellent with me. After you deliver the money, I have some errands to do before we leave for the trip," Jason replied.

"That's fine. Remember what I told that you, you would not go anywhere by yourself. Cyrus will drive you, and he will be with you at all times. Now, let us get some sleep. We have a long day ahead of us tomorrow," said Richard.

Chapter 6
The Sleep Over

Everybody slowly proceeded to their rooms. Rita walked toward Jason and said, "I anticipate you know what you are doing? If you do something thoughtless, they will seriously hurt you, or even worse, they will kill you. When my dad said that Cyrus would kill you, he meant it."

"Don't worry; I know perfectly well what I am doing. I am not foolish. I am a penniless and homeless man, but not stupid. I'm a man of principle. I always keep my promise," Jason replied.

Cyrus was waiting for Jason in the living room with the pillows and blankets. He asked Jason where he wished to sleep. "The floor is just fine. I probably wouldn't get a good night's sleep on a soft mattress, anyway," Jason replied.

Jason situated the pillows on the floor and attempted to find a comfortable position. He tried to sleep, but he could not even close his eyes. He lay back intently gazing at the ceiling. He could not believe what had really happened to him that night. He could not sleep and Cyrus snoring made it more impracticable for him to sleep. Very anxious, Jason got up from the floor and sat on a chair.

After a period of time, he walked to the kitchen and made himself a cup of coffee. Jason was trying to wisely decide what he was going to do with all the money. He had a good strategy for the treasure, but everything happened so fast. Jason conceived he needed some time by himself to fully clarify his plan.

It was not long after, Rita walked into the kitchen also. She turned the lights on, "Oh shit. You scared the hell out of me. What are you doing in the dark?" she asked Jason.

"You could not sleep also?" Jason asked Rita.

"No. This is ample intense excitement for me in one night," she replied.

"Do you want some coffee?" Jason asked her.

"Please," politely she answered.

Jason slowly poured her a cup of coffee, handed it to Rita and they both giggled. The giggling woke Cyrus. "Listen to you two; I would like to get some sleep," muttered Cyrus from the living room, where he was sleeping.

"Aren't you nervous that Jason might run away tonight while you are sleeping?" Rita asked Cyrus.

"He'd better not or something really bad could actually happen to his girlfriend. How do you expect me to sleep with all those lights on?" said Cyrus.

"Stop snoring and you will sleep even better," Rita replied. Rita asked Cyrus if it were all right for Jason and her to go in the back room. "That is fine, as long as you keep your eye on him. Just always remember I hate to be the one to tell your father that Jason tried to sexually assault you, and you fell down the stairs and broke your neck while running away from him," replied Cyrus in a treating manner. Jason did not welcome the threat Cyrus made towards Rita and himself. He stood up and commenced to walk towards where Cyrus was in the living room. Rita held him behind. She turned the kitchen lights off, and both went to the rear room. Sitting in the room with the lights dim Rita started to speculate how Jason knew so much about the caves. She made two cups of coffee, sat down on the chair beside Jason.

"Why do you know so much about the island of Melita? How do you know from the description on the map, without even seeing it yet?" she asked Jason.

Jason gave Rita a smile and said, "Wow. That's lots of questions. It's a long story."

"And we have a long night," Rita said with a smile.

"I'll tell you. You see, I was born on the island named Melita. The only reason no one can find Melita on any maps, unless you have an accident map like the one your father found, is because the name was changed to Mal." And he stopped.

"To Mal?" asked Rita. "It changed to what?" she asked again.

At the same time as Rita and Jason were having this conversation, Cyrus got up, sneaked to the back room and remained behind the door carefully listening to what Jason and Rita were talking about. Besides, he hadn't much great confidence in Rita ever since she took Jason's deep interest in every disagreement they had.

"I am sorry. It's not that I don't fully trust you, but you know there is lots of money involved here and not mentioning the millions of dollars that your father will receive after the discovery. I will tell you the name at the right time. That's best for everybody," said Jason.

"That's okay," answered Rita. "I fully understand."

"Where was I?" Jason continued. "Oh, the name Melita was altered to what it is called now. I eventually became an educator at the young age of twenty two."

"Really, that's funny. I am also a teacher," said Rita. "What subject do you teach, or should I say, did you teach?" she asked.

"History, I love history. Since I was six years old, I still can remember regularly visiting the historical places all around Melita with my father. Every time I explored these historic momentous I pictured myself living throughout those days. The school teaching job did not last too long. The government controlling education, the cutbacks and being a young teacher did not help the circumstances. I lost my job, and I could not come across any other profession. The declining economy of the island was very bad, and many citizens on the island were losing their jobs. Quite a few residents migrated to other countries looking for a better future. In my spare time, which I had lots of, I visited the public museums and studied about the history of this island. Everything I studied about, I did research for my profound knowledge."

Jason stopped; he gently rubbed his teary, tired eyes.

"Is that how you know about the golden bird?" asked Rita.

"No, no, I know only about the cave and its whereabouts. No one has ever been in Hassan's cave. It's about four hundred feet on top the sea level," replied Jason. "When you live on an island with such considerable historical events, the majority of the people will not pay any attention to everything there is to know. They take everything for granted. It is there to see it when you want to, but you never do. In regard to the cave, I read about it. I did research; I discovered it myself. It is extremely difficult to reach the top of cave without the proper equipment," finished Jason.

"How did you know that the bird is worth awful lots of money?" Rita, who was getting fascinated in the story, asked.

"It was over five hundred years ago when there was a holy war engaging between the Muslims and the Christians. The Turks attempted to take over Melita that was all Christians. At that time, Melita was under the protection of Spain that was also Christians. The Spanish armada was very dominant. They overpowered the Turks, and when the holy war was over, and the Turks withdrew. The Spanish government liked to give to the people of the island a contribution for their outstanding bravery and for the worthy assistance; they gave to the Spanish armada. The king himself offered to the grand master of the island a golden statue of a bird. The bird symbolizes the freedom on the island. The golden bird was stolen from the grand master's palace, and no one ever saw the bird statue again."

"Well, why does the map show the bird hidden in the cave?" Rita asked.

Jason was getting tired. "During the violent conflict, one of the Turkish generals was actually apprehended. While he was in solitary confinement, he actively collaborated with the Spanish generals and generously gave them plots of military intelligence about the Turks' plans. He wisely decided to work together with the Spanish generals to avert execution. He came to be friendly with the grand master so much that he was permitted to live in the grand master's palace as a trusted servant. When the crusade was over, the King of Spain went to Melita to present the golden bird to the citizens of Melita. The captive stole the golden bird from the official residence and ran away. No one ever saw him or the bird statue again. The escaped prisoner's name, who stole the statue, was Hassan. He made direct connection with some of the Turks who deserted during the war; they decided to actively remain on the island. After a couple of months of Hassan's break out from the palace, young females began suddenly to vanish from the island. It has been told that Hassan and his group kidnapped these youthful females and held them confined in a cave. This is the same cave that your father is looking for. Ships came in throughout in the hours of darkness to take the adult females to other kingdoms and auctioned as slaves. No one ever actually saw the ships coming in, up to the time until one night, when a farmer saw a ship sailing in. It was uncommon to see any kind of sea vessel sailing in that vicinity and close to the rocks. The farmer couldn't control his curiosity. He deliberately moved closer and hid behind a large rock. He remained motionless because he was very frightened. After a brief moment, he saw females getting roped down from the cave onto the ship. He was completely nervous, yet he remained behind the rock observing and awaited until the ship sailed out. He ran to the nearest farm house to get some help, but no one would believe his story. The next morning before sunrise, the farmer rode his horse to the capital and told the grand master of what he saw. The grand master commanded the knights to escort the farmer to his village and for them to maintain oversee around the area. The first night that the knights stand on guard, they saw a youthful man mounting up from the cave. The guards without any slight hesitation ran after the young man and properly secured him. This man was interrogated by the guards, but he declined to collaborate. He simply refused to give the guards his name; he kept quiet. One of the guards climbed down the rope, entered the cave and found four young women securely fastened inside the cave. The guards transported the women up to safety and set them free. The man whom they captured was taken to the grand master's palace.

"To the grand master's absolute astonishment, he identified the young man and ordered the guards to execute the man called Hassan." Jason started to get tired but Rita wanted to hear more.

"That is a very intense story, but how has the map got to Spain?" Rita asked.

Jason, half asleep, said, "According to the legend, when Hassan stole the bird statue, he hid it in the cave, and properly drafted the maps of the treasure's exact location. There are two ways to the cave entrance; one is to climb up about four hundred feet from the water level. You required being a good climber to be able to do that. The other way is the one on the map, but you still have to do some climbing to get to the main cave. It is not easy, each way. The map exhibits the simplest way to the cave entrance. After Hassan stole the golden statue, he drew the maps and had them dispatched to one of his acquaintances in Turkey, on one of the ships that at random picked up the younger women. The ship vanished in a severe storm. Anyway, your father is going to be well-known after the discovery and very rich too," expressed Jason, as he stood up to get to the living room to get some sleep.

"This is going to be very fascinating to witness," Rita said while she lightly rubbed her exhausted eyes.

"Why don't you go and get some sleep?" Jason recommended to Rita.

"Yes. That is a good idea. See you in the morning," Rita replied. Cyrus was carefully listening of the whole time, and ran back to his sleeping place. He got more excited after he clearly heard what Jason had said and could hardly wait to get his plan into action.

Rita went back to her room, and Jason lay on the floor and fell asleep. That was Jason's first night in a rather long time that he slept indoors, with a roof over his head and the gentleness of a pillow under his head. He could feel the tenderness of the blanket over him. Jason happily thought back of when he was a young kid and getting tucked in bed by his mother every night.

Chapter 7
Jason's Past

The sun's bright light shined on Richard's bedroom window. He got out of bed, showered and went rushing downstairs. He was pondering whether Jason bailed out on him and ran away. On his way to the kitchen, he noticed that Jason wasn't in the living room sleeping. Everybody was still sleeping, other than Jason, who was sitting at the kitchen table. Richard entered into the kitchen looked at Jason, in a sort of bizarre way.

"Why are you looking at me like that?" Jason asked.

"I thought that you would be gone by now," Richard softly whispered.

"Why should I walk away from a great fortune? Besides, I have a score to settle with your boy, Cyrus," said Jason with a smile.

"Listen, kid. You had excellent opportunity to leave last night. No one was going to stop you. You still have the occasion to back off because if you betrayed me, I will look for you; I will find you, and I will kill you myself," said Richard while he poured himself a cup of coffee. "Do you want some more coffee?" Richard asked Jason.

"Yes, if you please. Why do you want me to leave? Without me, you'll never find that treasure you're looking for," replied Jason.

"I already told you, if you are deceitful and take us on a wild goose chase, I swear to god. I will kill you. That is, if Cyrus doesn't kill you before I do," said Richard with a half smile.

"I very well know. You strongly related that already," Jason replied. He continued "But I am not lying, and I am not going to run away. I just want you to fully trust me," said Jason as he slowly sipped some coffee.

While Jason and Richard were sitting quietly in the kitchen drinking their coffee, gazing at each other without saying a word, Cyrus strolled in.

He looked at Jason and said, "Oh, you are still over here. I am quite astonished. I do not know if you are that intelligent or that brainless. You had your chance, bum, to leave; now reality will sink in. You will have to face all the outcomes if you screw up."

Jason stood up, looked at Cyrus, and told him, "You sure talk a lot first thing in the morning," and he walked out of the kitchen.

"Yes, he is still here. Now drink your coffee and shut up," Richard yelled at Cyrus.

Jason was walking away from the kitchen when Rita was on her way in. "Good morning, Jason. How did you sleep last night?" she asked.

"With my eyes closed," comically Jason replied.

Rita walked in the kitchen and said good morning to Cyrus, and she gave her father a gentle kiss. "What time are we going to the bank?" Cyrus asked Richard.

Richard had to ask Rita what time the banks opened because since he was always sailing Richard didn't know what the working hours on any establishments were. She told him that normally the banks opened at around ten o'clock. Richard told Cyrus to bring the car out of the garage, so they could go to the bank. On his way out the door, Cyrus asked Richard if he wanted him to bring his gun.

"That's a lot of cash, boss, to carry all over the city," Cyrus informed Richard.

"No requirement for a gun, just go bring the car," Richard told Cyrus.

Cyrus shook his head, and shouted loudly from downstairs intended for Samantha to get down, and he continued his way to the car garage. He drove the car to the front of the driveway. Richard and Samantha strolled down the doorway and got to the car. Midway down the driveway, Richard walked back to the house and notified Rita to arrange that Jason take a shower at the same time they were gone. "Give him a few of my outfits to change into. He cannot be seen walking with me appearing like that. Maintain an eye on him while we are gone." Richard headed back to the car. Jason, standing in front of the living room window, watched Cyrus driving away. A million deep thoughts were going in his mind; standing still he began the set up for his vengeance.

As soon as her father had departed, Rita walked close to Jason. "You heard my dad. You need to take a shower and change into some clean clothes." Jason calmly told Rita that he was no sudden rush and that Richard has to wait for him. Rita slightly shrugged her shoulders and asked Jason if something was troubling him. Jason told her that he was tremendously fine and went sat down on the chair. Rita could see that Jason was up to something by the strange expression on his face.

"Tell me," Rita questioned Jason. "Why and how did you become...you know..." Rita paused

"A bum?" Jason suddenly interrupted.

"Well, sort of. You basically know what I mean. I don't want to hurt your feelings," replied Rita modestly.

Jason smiled, and told Rita that she knows more about his life than himself.

"After I concluded my teaching job I could not stumble on any work. Visiting the museums and historical sites gave me a little time to think in relation to myself. Day after day, I often wondered what my foreseeable future would be. I kept asking myself if I was ever going to come across any work. I was applying for any category of work. At that time, employment conditions were extremely horrific. To maintain my brain positively active I did volunteer work at one of the museums. One day, while I was doing my primary responsibilities at the museum, a fairly young woman slowly approached me. She asked me a question regarding a marble statue from the Roman era. The minute I looked at her, I momentarily froze. I just could not respond to her question. She was very attractive; she had big dark eyes, long black silky hair. I just kept steadily gazing at her. She lightly shakes me from my shoulders and asked me if I was alright. Totally humiliated, my face turned red with total embarrassment. I apologized to her, and I told her that I had never been in the presence of such a very attractive young lady. Shocking to both of us, she also had the curiosity about the island history; we spent the entire afternoon discussing the island history. We got together more often." Jason briefly hesitated for a moment, stood up and walked towards the window.

"We became extremely emotionally involved with each other. Each time we saw one another, I was in high spirits but at the same time, I became quite depressed. It just did not look like entirely fair to her. I was out of work, and she had a secure, full time profession. She was beautiful, and I didn't justify such attractiveness around me."

"What category of work did she do?" asked Rita.

Jason twisted in the order to face Rita. "She worked for the government immigration agency," Jason replied. "One night, we met and the minute I saw her, I perfectly well knew that something was seriously wrong. She didn't have that affectionate smile, and her hand was cold. I asked her if something was greatly troubling her. With tears running down her face, she informed me that she was being transferred to Canada to work at the council for the immigrants of the island that are residing in Canada. I felt like someone put a dagger into my heart. I looked at her, held her hands and gave her a kiss and walked away in tears. She called my name. I pretended that I didn't hear her, I kept walking. Suddenly, I heard her footsteps following me. Her hand touched mine, and she begged me to stop. 'This is not the end of us; this could be the new being of us forever,' she told me, and then she asked me if I loved her. With tears in my eyes I told her that I passionately loved her so much. She said that the government would consent to us traveling together if we were married. I happily started to cry and laugh at the same time.

"Two days later, we got married. After six months after our wedding, we left the island and arrived in Canada. When we arrived in Canada, we had a permanent residence of our own to live in. It was not difficult for me to come across a job. By no means had I seen so many prospects in my life. Our life was starting to appear for the better than it was the previous year. The year after we arrived in Canada; we had a baby girl. It was six months after Tanya was born when the entire world ended for me and crumbled. One snowy evening I finally returned home from work. When I entered I called her name like I typically did, there was no response. I ran upstairs, they were gone. She took my baby and ran away. I became fanatical. I looked all over for them. I asked her friends, but no one knows, or at least they didn't want to tell what had happened to them. I inquire her employer; her co-workers. Nobody knows wherever she went, or whatever happened to her and the baby. Lastly, I went to the police station, but they could not help me either. I went back to the house, I cried for hours. I rummaged around every room for any clues. Nothing, I did not find anything. She did not even leave me a note. She took all her clothes and the baby clothes all the money that we saved together. A few weeks later I received a letter from her. She told me that she went back to the island, and that she could not live with me any longer. She did not give me any compelling reasons or what if whatever thing wrong that I did.

"She told me she just simply wanted to be on her own.

"What hurts the most was when she told me not to be troubled going back to look for them. I was traumatized. I started drinking a great deal of booze. I was absent from work; I was terminated from my job. I attempted to look for work again, but nobody wished to employ me.

"I became a chronic alcoholic. I moved from city to city. I would find a job and lose it again. I just could not somehow manage the excessive consumption of the alcohol. I officially applied for an American visa and moved to Detroit. By then, the rescession was all over, tried to look for work but nothing was available. I kept slowly drifting from state to state, from city to city, until I arrived in California. It has been over ten years that I had been living here." Jason was getting deeply emotional.

"Why did you stay here in California?" Rita asked.

"The type of weather is somewhat similar to where I came from. For a person in my current situation with no bed to sleep on and a place to stay, except for the alleys, night time can get very cold. You know that this was my first night that I have slept under a roof in the past ten years." Jason stopped short as he scratched his filthy beard.

"Now, what are you going to do with my dad's money?" Rita politely enquired.

"First of all, it's not your dad's money. To let know you the truth, I don't know. I have not for a moment seen that much money in my entire existence. I will do my most excellent to assist your dad to explore for the golden bird," Jason answered.

"Jason, make me happy and, truthfully, tell me that you are not going to be disloyal to my dad. You do not clearly understand what they can do to you. You have seen Cyrus's personality. He is very faithful to my dad, and he will not allow one to humiliate my dad," Rita begged to Jason. "My sincere judgment, I think Cyrus is mad. I don't know how my father ever got so mixed up with that man," Rita said while she got up from the sofa and walked towards the window.

Jason looked at Rita and said, "With no disrespect, your father is no archangel either. I have no quarrel with your dad, and I will definitely establish to you and Richard that I am a man of my word. Cyrus is different circumstances. I will painstakingly teach him a lesson. He thinks that I am stupid. I'll show him," Jason said with bitter anger.

"Now be alert when you're with him. I don't like him also," Rita said. "I suppose you better go and take a shower before they return. I will get a hold of some of my dad's clothes to wear for now." Rita went to Richard's room to look for some clothing for Jason to wear. Jason ran up the stairs and took a shower. He wore the clothes that Rita left hanging on the bathroom doorknob. When Jason came downstairs Rita looked at Jason with astonishment, and she asked, "Why didn't you shave or at least trim your beard?"

"I will later. We have other serious things to concern about," Jason replied.

"You know what? You look rather handsome in those clothes. They look far better on you than they do on my father," complimented Rita as they together laughed. Jason told Rita to stop the compliments because she was making him self-conscious. Jason went to sit down on the chair in front of the window. Jason saw Richard's car parking in the driveway.

Chapter 8
The Reward Money

Richard stamped out from the car in a great hurry, holding the briefcase with the money, Cyrus and Samantha pursued, and as soon as he entered the house he immediately walked up to Jason. "Well, you're still here! I had to do a lot of paperwork to get all this cash for you. Half-million dollars. Is that correct? You still have the opportunity to walk out of here and totally disregard this bargain, if you're thinking of being deceitful to me." Richard, holding the briefcase firm, told Jason.

"No, sir. I am a man who keeps his promise," answered Jason, at the same time he reached out for the briefcase.

"Not so fast," Cyrus yelled, and got in the middle of Jason and Richard. Cyrus looked at Jason, pressed his fist into Jason's chest and told him in a roughly treating manner, "You will be mine. Do you fully comprehend? Let me tell you, bum; once you put your filthy hands on this money you are a condemned man. I will be with you wherever you go. A word of utmost caution, one wrong move, and you are a dead man," finished saying Cyrus in a fuming voice.

"I don't like you also, mister. Before this joint expedition is over one of us..." Jason was rudely interrupted by Rita.

"Stop it, both of you. This is ridiculous," Rita interfered. "We all have to work jointly if we want to accomplish and to be successful in finding this treasure."

"That's right, now we are a team, and we have to bond together so we all benefit," Richard said while he grabbed Jason and Cyrus from their shoulders.

"Boss, I still say you are making a considerable mistake," Cyrus still insisted as he tried to take the briefcase away from Jason. "What happens if we don't find this golden statue? Does he get to keep the money?" Cyrus was very envious because he was by no means treated the way Jason was being treated fairly by Richard.

"The mutual agreement is for me to get you to Hassan's cave. What you do when I get you there is up to you people. Whether you'll find it or not, that money is mine," said Jason, and he grabbed the briefcase. "I rightfully assume this is mine," said Jason, while he pulled the briefcase from Cyrus's hand.

"Jason, are you going to carry all that money with you all the time?" Samantha asked.

"Don't worry about the money. I have some unfinished business to do first. I have to go to a bank and deposit this money and have it directly transferred to a bank in Melita," Jason said as he started heading towards the door.

"Not so fast, bum boy," Cyrus called as he ran to stop Jason from walking out the door. "Do you have undersized recollection? Where do you think you are going by yourself?" Cyrus asked while he pulled Jason back inside.

"Who is the dummy around here? Did I just finish saying that I have to go to a bank to make a deposit?" Jason replied smiling.

"Didn't I tell you already once before that you were not going anywhere by yourself," Cyrus said, and he stepped towards Jason.

"That's right. We had an agreement. Cyrus told you, and I kept warning you. Once you fully accepted the money you became my property and you belong to me," said Richard.

"I guess you did say that, and I fully acknowledged. Let's go then," said Jason. Before Jason could step outside Cyrus pulled Jason back and clearly warned him that if he tried to run away from him, he would shoot him. To really frighten Jason, Cyrus opened his jacket and showed Jason the gun.

"Cyrus, I am a man of my word. I always keep my pledge and bear that in mind. Now that we clearly identify with each other, can you take me to a bank?" Jason asked. Cyrus escorted Jason to the car. Cyrus asked Jason where they were going to.

"I require going to the public library on Main Street," replied Jason. Cyrus told Jason to sit in the back seat. Jason stood by the car door and waited. Cyrus asked what he was waiting for. "Aren't you going to open the door for me?" Jason asked.

Cyrus wasn't in a joking mood and told Jason that if he didn't get in the car, then he would throw him in.

Sitting in silence at the back seat of the car, Jason began planning his sweet revenge that will teach Cyrus a lesson, and at the same time he would get Richard's complete confidence.

Back at Rita's home, Richard seemed fairly peaceful sitting on the divan. His thoughts were about the golden statue. He was slightly anxious for the day to come when he would be the proud owner of such treasure. He called Rita and asked her to sit beside him. He told her that he wished her to go with them to this island. Since Rita had never traveled with her dad she got in high spirits since she was always engaged in schooling.

Rita warmly embraced her dad and told him "Of course, dad. I wouldn't miss this for the world. Besides, I need a vacation," replied Rita cheerfully.

"You know that you have to get some time away from your teaching job," Richard reminded her.

"Yes, I know, dad. Once you decide when we are leaving, I will have to give the school my request for a leave of absence," said Rita and gave her father a kiss on his forehead.

Samantha kept to herself all this time and never actively engaged in any of the urging. She kept thinking of what Cyrus had told her that he had a plan for the treasure. Nevertheless, what kind of plan did Cyrus have? Cyrus never discussed in detail with Samantha any of his plans, she was sitting on the sofa daydreaming.

Richard looked at her and asked her if she was okay. Samantha did not reply. Richard got up and shook her from her shoulders; he asked her again if she was all right.

"Yes, I am okay," she replied.

"You look very worried, my darling," said Richard.

"No, I am not worried. Why should I be worried? I'm just a bit confused," Samantha said in a low voice.

"Confused," laughed Richard. "You were born confused."

Samantha got very upset with Richard. She stood up, turned to Richard and slapped him in the face. "You are not at any time nice to me. I hope that bum will run with your money and never come back," Samantha yelled at Richard.

Richard stopped laughing and firmly grasped Samantha's shoulders and in a heated voice said, "You ever do that to me again, and I will rip your head apart. If that bum runs away with my money, what do you suppose that I will do to your lover?"

Samantha got uneasy when Richard called Cyrus her lover. She ran upstairs and locked the door behind her. Lying on the bed, Samantha was deeply troubled.

She started to visualize if Richard knew about her and Cyrus having sex together behind his back. If he did know, what would he do to them? Samantha had no loyalty to Richard or Cyrus, especially now that Jason was implicated. He had at least half a million dollars to himself. All Cyrus had was a plan and no money. Jason had a half a million dollars, and when the search was over, he would be a million dollars richer. That was only a small fraction of what Richard had, but now she was terrified and concerned that Richard would seriously harm her. What future would Cyrus and Samantha have if Richard separated from both? They had no money and no place to stay. She had to do a great deal of planning, whether she should stay with Richard and all his money and to be anxious for the rest of her life. Perhaps Richard called Cyrus as her lover just to see her initial reactions; after all, Cyrus and Samantha were alone on the yacht for almost a month.

Should she stay with Cyrus and only hope that his plan will work, or should she try to get to be close friends with Jason. She did not know what she should work at. She went downstairs, made herself a drink of rum and went back to her room.

Back downstairs, Rita had also had some critical thinking of her own. She was not thinking about money, but about Jason. Is he telling the truth? Does he sincerely know where the golden bird is? What does Jason truly look like without his beard? Will Jason run away? All of this was going throughout Rita's mind. She kept speculating what Jason would do after the search is over. She started to become affectionate toward Jason, because of the rugged life he had, or because of his straightforward personality.

Richard sat totally relaxed, with nothing at all to worry about. He was considering himself holding that golden bird and the entire splendour he would have when he discovered the treasure. Richard turned to Rita and asked her, "Rita, did he briefly indicate anything to you where we are going to find this bird, or where Melita is?"

"No, but he had a rough life, the poor man; I honestly feel remorseful for him," said Rita.

"Just in case you've forgotten, he has half a million dollars of my money, and I have zero to show for it," Richard reminded Rita.

"Yes, but look at the bright side; when you find that gold statue you are going to be at least five hundred million dollars richer and very famous. You are worried about a half million for all his trouble," answered Rita.

"Well let me guess; you're having some personal appeal for this bum," asked Richard.

"A bum? At the moment, he is a bum. First, you called him a kid, now a bum; you have got no judgment for nobody," said Rita in a mad voice and walked away.

Richard got up from the sofa; he asked her to stop. "Look at us. We are fighting when we should be feasting," Richard told Rita.

"I'm sorry, dad. I didn't mean to raise my voice," Rita replied. "Yes, I do have some special fondness for him," she said as her face became red.

"I'm remorseful for all the trouble that we caused. If Jason is honest, I will take good care of him," replied Richard. They both hugged. It didn't take Cyrus long, sooner than they showed up at the library.

Chapter 9
The Revenge

Cyrus parked the car in front of the library main entrance. Jason told Cyrus that it might take him about an hour to glance for what he required. Jason grabbed his backpack, opened the car door and stepped out of the car and easily reached out for the briefcase.

"Not so fast," called out Cyrus as he pulled the gun to Jason's face. "The money stays here with me for security; besides, you don't need any money for the library, do you bum boy?"

"This is my cash," Jason responded.

"Not yet. Not until we get to the bank," Cyrus told Jason.

"All right," said Jason while gradually, gently pushing the gun away from his face. "Fine, you don't have to get extremely anxious. If it makes you feel better, I will leave the briefcase here in the car. You will be fully responsible if anything happens to the money. It is that okay with you?" Jason asked Cyrus.

"Yes, that will make me feel a lot better. Now get moving and don't take long," ordered Cyrus. Jason kept his calm, stepped away from the car, and closed the door behind him. Carrying the backpack on his shoulder walked towards the library entrance.

He did not look behind to see if Cyrus was still surveying him. Cyrus didn't take his eyes off Jason until Jason entered the library. As soon as Jason entered, he fast approached the receptionist and asked her how he could get to the back exit.

"Why do you want to use the back exit; you just entered from the front door?" she asked.

"There is a man outside in a red car, and he has been following me around. I think he is trying to do harm to me, and I am afraid," said Jason with a worried look on his face.

The receptionist asked Jason if he wanted her to call the police. He told her not to, and she asked him to follow her to the back door.

She took him to the back emergency exit door. She opened the door for him, and he stepped out into to the back alley. The alleys were not out of the ordinary to Jason; he knew them like the back of his hand, there he felt at home. He thanked the woman and walked away. Jason had his own effective strategy, and this was Cyrus's first lesson.

Back in the car, Cyrus was waiting patiently for almost two hours, waiting for Jason to return. Cyrus automatically presumed the only reason Jason eagerly sought after the money in cash was so he could run away with the money. He knew that the bum did not know anything about where the treasure was, neither where the island of Melita was. Jason planned to steal the money, and that's what he did just like Cyrus thought. He got tired waiting impatiently for Jason to return; he got out of the car and headed for the library. He looked just about everywhere and could not see Jason anywhere. Cyrus approached the receptionist; he told her that his brother had called him to pick him up. Cyrus gave her a brief description of Jason and asked her if she had seen him. The receptionist told Cyrus that she remembered the fellow. She informed Cyrus that he had left a while ago. The receptionist told Cyrus that someone was following him, and that he was pretty scared. She also told Cyrus that he went out from the back door. Cyrus smiled and thanked her, told the receptionist perhaps that's why he had called him. Cyrus thanked the lady and walked back to the car. As soon as he entered the car, he said to himself that he knew that Jason was a crook. Cyrus reached to the back seat for the briefcase. He grabbed the briefcase, and the second he lifted the briefcase up, he got tense. The briefcase weighed lighter. He quickly opened the briefcase and, to his bewilderment, the briefcase was relatively empty. All the money was gone, and so was Jason.

Cyrus did not know what to do. At that single instant, he wished that he had killed Jason when he had the excellent opportunity. Jason had an almost two-hour head start on him, and where was Cyrus going to start looking for Jason? Cyrus started to panic and heavily perspire, because he did not know how he was going to give an explanation of what happened to the money to Richard.

Cyrus sat in the car thinking of many excuses to tell Richard, but couldn't come up with any. Unhurriedly, he drove to Rita's house; his heart was pounding fast, and he started to tremble. When he arrived at Rita's house, he walked slowly with the empty briefcase in his hand. He opened the door, and Richard was waiting for them to return. Cyrus stood in the hallway with the briefcase in his hand; he wasn't the same old self.

"What's wrong with you?" Rita questioned when she saw Cyrus standing still in the corridor. By the look on the Cyrus's face, she could tell that something bad had happened.

Richard stepped into the corridor, looked at Cyrus, and said, "What is wrong with you? What did you do with Jason? Where in the hell is he?" Richard yelled at Cyrus.

The way Cyrus appeared, Richard knew that something was terribly wrong.

"He, he is gone. He ran away," Cyrus answered as he leant against the corridor wall.

"Gone? Gone where? What do mean he ran away? I'll be damned. He screwed me up. Now he knows what we are looking for, and he knows where to search for the treasure. Dummy me, and I started to trust him," said Richard in a humble voice.

"Well, let's take this money back to the bank," Richard ordered. "He can't get too far, especially without any money, and he still requires a passport to go to the island of Melita. I have strong connections at the passport office, and I am going to make sure that he won't be able to leave the state, let alone the United States."

"Umn, um, boss," stuttered Cyrus as he started to speak. "There is something I have to tell you."

"And what is that?" Richard asked with annoyance.

"The money boss, he took the money," replied Cyrus trembling.

"What?" yelled Richard. "How could he take the money when you have the briefcase in your hand and only you and I have the keys to open it?"

"He must have opened the briefcase while we were on our way to the library and stacked away the money in his backpack. I found this nail file on the back seat. He was going to take the briefcase with him inside, but I told him to leave the money with me in the car while he went into the library." Cyrus stopped talking because his mouth was completely dried up.

Richard ran towards Cyrus and threw a punch at Cyrus. Cyrus fell down. Richard started booting Cyrus all over his body. Cyrus was loudly screaming for assistance and pleaded Richard to stop. Rita heard the yelling and ran towards them. She got in between and roughly pushed her dad away. Samantha heard the yelling also and ran downstairs. She was distressed when saw Cyrus's body lying on the floor with a bloody face. Cyrus's body was almost immobile; Samantha knelt down and called Cyrus's name a few times, and he did not react to her calling. Rita got angry and told Richard to get out of her house. Richard walked out the door, slamming it on his way out.

Rita was hit with intense horror as she couldn't believe what just had occurred in her house; what once was a peaceful house. Cyrus began to progress by moving his arms slowly. Rita and Samantha assisted him up to his feet. Rita proposed to Cyrus and Samantha to stay at her house up to the time that Cyrus got slightly better. Rita angrily demanded that they had to leave when Cyrus healed and never wanted to see them and her dad ever again. Rita and Samantha helped Cyrus to walk to the upstairs bedroom. Samantha went down to the kitchen and got an ice pack to put on Cyrus's face while Rita washed the blood off his face. Cyrus's face was bruised and badly swollen from Richard's beating, and he could not open his eyes. He lay in bed, unbearably painful.

"How are you feeling?" Samantha asked him while she put an ice bag on his face.

"I am going to kill them both; I swear," said Cyrus while holding his ribs in pain.

"What are we going to do now?" Samantha asked as she started to cry.

"We have to go back to Richard. I told him not to trust that bum, and he held me solely responsible for his stubbornness. We have to find that bum before he leaves the country. He knows too much about the treasure," Cyrus said in sheer misery.

Two weeks went by, and Cyrus was feeling better. He asked Rita to call her father to tell him that he would like to talk to him, and that they had to find Jason. Richard had spent the last two weeks on his yacht alone; he did not feel safe and sound on his yacht all by himself, which was when he realized how absolutely essential Cyrus was to him.

Richard received the call from Rita and told her that he would visit Cyrus. It was not long after he received the call from Rita that Richard arrived at her house. When Rita opened the door for him, she formally instructed her dad that she did not want any more problems. Richard solemnly promised her that he wouldn't cause any.

Cyrus and Richard looked at each other as Cyrus began to speak. "We'll have to find him. He knows too much, and we don't want him to sell the crucial information to anyone else," Cyrus said.

"You mean you are not pissed off at me?" Richard asked.

"Of course not. If someone stole half a million dollars from me, I would have done the same thing, but then again, I don't have half a million dollars," said Cyrus.

Samantha could not figure out what was going through Cyrus's mind. Two weeks ago, he wanted to kill Richard, and now he wanted to help Richard to find Jason. Richard and Cyrus shook hands and decided to work together to find Jason.

Rita smiled, and made drinks for all four of them. "I agree; he has to be found. He got me easily fooled as well. You must find him. He almost shattered your friendship," Rita said as she went to the kitchen.

"Not just our friendship, but my bank account too," Richard replied with a smile.

Cyrus asked Richard if he had called his contact at the passport office. Richard replied that thus far no one by Jason's name applied for a passport. Rita came out from the kitchen, turned to her dad and told him that Jason could not have an American passport because he was a Canadian citizen. Richard easily explained to her that with the correct quantity of money and with the exact contact, Jason could have any passport he wanted. Let's not forget all the money he has. The four of were trying to figure out a plan to locate Jason.

Chapter 10
Jason's Hiding

What ever happened to Jason? Why did he run away with the money? His first aim was to firmly establish himself to Richard that he could be trusted. Secondly, he wanted to get even with Cyrus for all the harassing he had to put up with from him. On the way to the library, Jason opened the briefcase with a nail file that he had taken from Rita's bathroom. He made sure that Cyrus did not see him. Then he stashed the money inside his back pack.

The first thing he wanted to do was to put the money in a safe place, but he had no idea where. He could not just walk into a bank and ask to deposit a half million dollars in cash, that would make everyone very wary. He kept reminding himself that he had to plan his upcoming step. He flipped a steel dustbin upside down and sat on it trying to outline what he was going to do next. "I have to get some new clothes, and I need to find a place to stay," Jason said to himself. He stood up and headed towards the beachfront area. He walked towards the first motel that he saw. He looked around making sure that Cyrus or Richard was not following him. He entered the motel and paid for a month stay. The motel clerk asked Jason for some kind of identification. Jason told the office clerk that he did not have any on him because his wife had kicked him out of the house and that all his belongings were still at the house. Jason pulled out a one hundred bill and exhibited it to the clerk and, without any hesitation, the clerk expressly confirmed the reservation for Jason. The motel clerk gave Jason the keys to room ten. Jason took the keys and told the clerk that he didn't want to be disturbed and went to his room.

Once he went inside his room, he laid down on the bed to rest. Staring at the low ceiling, he was desperately trying to figure out a way to get back to Richard before Richard caught up with him first and found Jason. If that happened, it would totally destroy everything for Jason and he would end up dead. Thus far, his plan had worked, but he had one big dilemma: where was he going to conceal all that money?

Jason got out of bed, cut a hole in the side of the mattress, and stuffed most of the money inside it. "I have to get new clothes. I can't go around in Richard's clothes because if they see me, I will be a dead man," Jason softly muttered to himself as he walked out of his room and locked the door behind him. On his way out, he told the clerk to make sure that nobody went into his room, and not to bother sending the house cleaner to clean it up.

Jason handed to the clerk a fifty dollar bill and walked out of the motel looking for a men's clothing store. He walked all along the pavement and when he suddenly spotted a wanderer sitting on the sidewalk, Jason turned to the drifter. Jason asked him if he was interested in trading clothes with him.

The drifter smiled and asked Jason, "Sure, but why?"

"Just don't ask any questions and let's get it over with," replied Jason. Jason changed into the drifter clothes, gave the drifter a fifty-dollar bill for his special consideration. Jason felt more at ease knowing that Cyrus or Richard wouldn't be looking for him dressed the way he was before, wearing Richard's clothes. He walked out of the alley and continued to look for a men's clothing store. There weren't any clothing stores at the beach area, so he walked to the downtown area, a few miles away from where he was. He entered into the first clothing store he saw. In a minute as he walked in the store, a shop assistant yelled at him and told him to get out of the store.

"I came to buy some new outfits," Jason told the sales clerk.

"I don't think we have any of your personal appearances," the shop assistant said to Jason with a smile, while he was very aggressive pushing Jason backwards towards the front door. Jason tried to push himself in and the shop assistant stepped in front of him and said, "Please go to another place before I call the police. Please, sir, go away," begged the sales clerk.

Jason was getting a little annoyed of being pushed around because of the way he was dressed. He grabbed the shop assistant by his shirt and told him to take him to the store manager.

The shop assistant started yelling for someone to help him. Jason told the shop assistant to take him to the store administrator. "Mr. Remington is occupied, and he won't be able to see you, sir," replied the shop assistant, scared stiff.

"I said, take me to him," yelled Jason while he shoved away the shop assistant up against the mirror. One of the other sales clerks suddenly tried to grab Jason from behind, but Jason saw him coming and rammed him down to the floor.

With the entire racket that was going on, the manager came out of his office.

"What is going on? Who is he? What is he doing in here?" Mr. Remington asked as he pointed towards Jason.

"Are you the manager?" Jason asked angrily.

"No, I'm the owner and the manager," he replied

"My name is Jason French. I came in here to buy some clothes. Your salesman simply refused to wait on me, and the other one tried to hit me from behind," Jason explained to Mr. Remington.

"Calm down and let my salesman go," Mr. Remington asked Jason.

"Do you want me to call the police, Mr. Remington?" asked the sales clerk.

"No, that won't be required. I will take care of this myself," replied Mr. Remington.

"Why don't you come into my office?" Mr. Remington asked Jason. They walked in the office, and Mr. Remington asked Jason to sit down. "Now, do you have any money? You know, you require money to buy clothing and this is not cheap clothing," said Mr. Remington.

Jason reached into his side pocket, and pulled out about two thousand dollars in cash and put it on the desk. He looked at Mr. Remington and asked, "Is this adequate?"

"More than just sufficient," Mr. Remington smiled. "Now tell me, what are you looking for? I am not going to be asking you where you got all that money," Mr. Remington said as he tried to pick up the money.

Jason grabbed the money and put back in his coat pocket. "I am looking for some pants, shirts, and shoes. I want the best in design," Jason replied.

Mr. Remington asked Jason to walk with him to the store. "May I ask where a person like you got such considerable amount of money?" he asked.

"I thought you told me that you don't care," Jason replied as they were walking out of Mr. Remington office.

Jason stopped, looked at Mr. Remington, and said, "Listen. First of all, it's none of your business and second." Jason hesitated a little because he did not know how to explain to Mr. Remington how he got the money. "I won it at the race track," continued Jason. "Big odds," expressed Jason, trying to stay calm.

"Okay, that's fine," replied Mr. Remington. "Now, if you tell me your size, I will personally help you out. What size?"

Jason answered. "It has been an extensive time since I bought me some new clothes, a very far reaching time."

"I know, I can tell," replied the Mr. Remington. "I'll go get the measuring tape."

Mr. Remington walked out of his office, and the two sales clerks asked him if he was okay. "Of course, you fool. You're both fired!" Mr. Remington yelled at them.

It took Jason around two hours to look for what he fancied. He asked Mr. Remington to have the clothes delivered to the motel. Mr. Remington, with all smiles, did not say no; furthermore, how often does a man spend over twenty-five hundred dollars on clothes in one day? Jason gave Mr. Remington the address of the motel where he was staying. Before he left the store, Jason dressed in one of the new outfits and went straight to the motel. As soon as he walked in he asked the clerk if anyone came looking for him.

"No, nobody," the motel clerk replied. "Are you actually expecting someone?

"Yes. I have a special delivery of new clothes I purchased to be delivered. If the delivery arrives when I am not here, put them on the bed and be careful with them," Jason said, and he went to his room. Jason opened the door and jumped onto the bed. He lay down and started to question himself what caused this change of luck, closed his eyes, and fell asleep. About half an hour later, the phone rang. Jason answered. "Sir, there is a man delivering your clothes, and he asked for room ten. Shall I send him in?" the motel clerk inquired.

"Yes, send him in," Jason replied; he hung up the phone.

He opened the door, and the deliveryman politely inquired where he would like him to put new outfits. "Put them on the bed for now," Jason answered.

The delivery man gently put Jason's clothes on the bed as he was instructed and left. "Next: step two," Jason said to himself. He shaved the beard, took a bath, and he put on one of the new suits he had just purchased. He looked at himself in the mirror and said, "I need a haircut." On his way out, the clerk didn't make out who he was. Jason called for a taxi, and before long the taxi arrived at the motel. Jason jumped in the back seat and told the driver to take him to the nearest barbershop.

After Jason walked out of the barbershop, he stopped, looked in the mirror, and appeared absolutely astonished by the major difference. "I don't even recognize myself," Jason said with a smile. Now, step three: the biggest step of them all. Jason told the taxi driver, which kept waiting outside while Jason had his haircut, to take him back to the motel.

Jason walked in, and the clerk asked him if he could help him.

"You fool, it's me, room ten," Jason replied.

The motel clerk looked at Jason, "Oh man, you look completely different. I didn't clearly distinguish you. I am sorry," humbly the clerk apologized.

Jason went to his room to get some cash, and got back in the taxi. He told the driver to proceed to Mandai Drive. Jason was seated in the back seat with an empty briefcase on his knees. He thought that it would make him more important-looking.

After about a twenty-minute drive, the driver told Jason, "This is Mandai Drive, sir. What's the number?"

Jason gave the driver Rita's house number. "Here we are, sir!" Jason paid the driver, got a hold of the briefcase and started to walk up the driveway towards the front door.

Chapter 11
Reunion

He knocked on the door; no one answered. He knocked again, this time harder. He felt very contented in his new look, and Jason was very much hoping that none of them would identify him.

"Wait, just a minute!" someone yelled from inside.

That was Rita, Jason said to himself. Suddenly, he started to get nervous. Rita opened the door, and asked, "Can I help you?"

"Hello. I am looking for Mr. Richard Nichols." Jason answered.

"Who are you?" Rita asked.

"I've got some facts concerning the man who ran away with a briefcase full of his money," Jason replied, as his self-confidence grew, knowing that Rita did not fully recognize him.

"Come in. I will let him know," Rita expressed. She ran upstairs and told her dad that there was man downstairs who had information about Jason. Richard, at that time, was having a conversation with Cyrus, and told Rita to let the man in. Richard, without any slight hesitation, ran down the stairs, and Cyrus and Samantha closely followed. Rita kindly invited Jason in. She had no idea that the man at the front door was Jason. Jason eagerly followed Rita to the living room where Richard was waiting anxiously.

"Who is he, and what does he want?" Richard asked, pretending that he had no interest in the man.

"Dad, this gentleman said that he had information for you," Rita informed Richard.

"Information, for me. What kind of information?" Richard asked.

"I've heard that you are missing a half million dollars?" Jason said.

"How do you know that?" all of a sudden interrupted Cyrus.

"Excuse me, but who are you?" Jason asked pleasantly.

"He is my bodyguard and my friend," Richard replied. Richard told Cyrus to sit down and to calm himself. Rita looked at Jason; he looked at her and asked Rita if there was something incorrect with him because she kept intently staring at him. She told him that there was basically nothing wrong with him. Rita continued telling Jason that he looked like someone she knew. Rita walked out from the living room and went in the kitchen, and her thoughts were about the man in the living room. She had a burning sensation that she met or knew that man from someplace "Something about that man is familiar," Rita said to herself.

"Mr. Nichols, I also know that you are looking for an expensive treasure. I have information of the precise location of Melita," Jason said.

"Well you know about a lot of stuff."

"Yes, sir, we have a good informant."

"Do you know that I am going to kick your teeth in?" Richard yelled, who began to lose his bad temper. "If you think that I am going to give you any money for your information, you are nuts. Just get the hell out of here," Richard yelled. Richard was pretending that he wasn't interested in what the man in front of him had to say.

Cyrus told Richard to be tranquil. He turned to Jason and asked him, "How do you know about the island of Melita?

"Just like your boss said, I am a good informant," Jason replied sarcastically. Jason walked towards Richard, looked him in his eyes and said, "Fifty bucks. For fifty bucks, I will tell you where you are able to find Jason. I know that you can come up with fifty dollars."

Rita was carefully listening from the kitchen, and came out and said," I'll give you one hundred dollars if you're right."

Richard interrupted; not letting Rita finished what she had to say. "You know his name too?" Richard asked.

"I told you, I know everything," Jason replied, mocking Richard.

"Here's fifty. Now tell me everything, starting with where I can find that bum." Richard asked, raising his voice.

Jason looked at Richard and said, "Your daughter generously offered me one hundred dollars." Richard reached in his pocket, and pulled out another fifty-dollar bill and handed the money to Jason.

Jason slowly grabbed the money from Richard's hand, looked at the four of them and said, "Mr. Nichols, Cyrus, Samantha, Rita; my name is Jason."

They all immediately started to cackle, except for Rita. "I knew it, there was something about you that looked familiar," Rita said.

"I had to firmly establish to you all that I can be trusted, and that fool that you call your main man is dim-witted," Jason said with a grin on his face.

Cyrus ran towards Jason and tried to punch him, but Jason was more than ready for him this time. Jason blocked off Cyrus's blow, and threw a strike at Cyrus and knocked him down.

"You see what I basically mean," Jason said. "He thinks that violent behaviour can settle everything." Cyrus dropped down to the floor, and everybody stopped smiling.

"You mean to tell me, that is you, bum?" asked Richard.

"Yes, this is me, in flesh and blood and brains," Jason replied as he looked down at Cyrus.

"Why did you come back, are you crazy?" Rita asked with interest.

"I told you all that I never break my promises to anybody," Jason replied.

"Yes, but you may perhaps have looked for the treasure yourself and turned into a richer man, since you already have half a million dollars of my money," Richard said to Jason.

"What am I going to do with all that money? It is your map, and you found it, we made a deal. You paid me half of the reward to lead you to Melita," Jason replied with sincere voice.

Rita walked towards Jason, gently hugged him, and said, "Remember that sleepless night when we were in the kitchen talking about your past? I knew that you are a different and perfectly honest man. Thank you for coming back," she told Jason.

"Oh, you are welcome," Jason replied with a smile.

With a grin on his face, Richard walked towards Jason and said, "In no way, in my life have I met up with a man like you."

"You see, like you said, I could have explored for the golden bird myself, and become very rich. It is your map and your treasure your finding. You compensated me upfront to take you and to lead you to find the treasure. I did what I did to reveal you that I can be trustworthy" Jason said.

"Don't be a fool," said Cyrus as he stood up. "This is another trick of his."

"Shut up. It wasn't me that got totally humiliated, remember," Richard told Cyrus.

Rita, overflowing with great pleasure, yelled out loud, "Let's commemorate this moment!" as she filled five glasses with wine and served each one.

Richard, Rita, and Samantha looked extremely pleased. Cyrus, he looked somewhat pleased. He tried to go cooperatively with the others, but vengeance was the only thing on his mind. He took the wine glass with him and walked out of the room, and Samantha quickly followed. Rita, Richard, and Jason were too content and did not even notice that Cyrus had left the room.

"Richard, I would like to make a special tribute," Jason said. He opened his briefcase and pulled out a bottle of champagne. Richard looked around, and he noticed that Cyrus and Samantha had left the room. Jason filled three glasses with champagne.

"What are we drinking for?" Richard asked with curiosity.

Chapter 12
The Falcon

"We are going to have a drink to the Maltese Falcon," Jason replied, and gently lifted his glass.

"What we are looking for?" Rita and Richard asked at the almost identical instant.

"You are looking for the Maltese Falcon, the most valuable and historical treasure in the world. Melita was the original name of the island. Years after the holy war ended the king of Spain altered the name of the island," said Jason.

"You mean to tell me that Melita is Malta?" Rita asked. "All the work I went through, and it is Malta?" she kept repeating to herself.

"Yes, once I read that ad in the newspaper; I knew precisely what you were after," Jason informed them.

Richard looked at Jason and asked him when is the earliest that they can start the search, so he can purchase the airfare tickets. Jason told Richard that they could not go by air because once they found the Falcon, they would not be legally capable of taking it out from the island. "You just can't hide it from the Maltese customs; additionally, it will be too heavy to carry around. We have to go with your yacht," Jason told Richard.

Jason briefly explained to Richard that they need a special apparatus to get to the top of the cave entrance, and that they will need ropes and a couple of inflatable dinghies.

Richard did not make any main arguments. "So it is. We'll go with the yacht."

He asked Rita if she be interested in order to go with them on the treasure hunt.

"I wouldn't bypass this for the world. Malta. I always cherished to visit there," Rita chuckled.

"We're going to require some unique provisions. I will make you a list of what we need. It is essential to have these provisions before we depart for Malta," Jason said, as he walked towards the front door.

"Wait. Where are you staying?" Rita asked Jason.

"I can't tell you, but how about lunch tomorrow?" Jason asked her.

Rita, full of great pleasure, asked Jason where they can meet and what time. He told her that he would be at her house at ten in the morning, and afterwards, they would decide what to do later.

He walked out the door and Rita ran upstairs. Halfway down the driveway, Jason suddenly remembered that he needed a ride back to the motel.

Jason walked back to the house and knocked on Rita's door.

"Wonder what that could be now?" mumbled Rita while she headed towards the front door.

She opened the door, and there was Jason on the doorstep. "Well, a foreigner, what can I do for you?" Rita joked.

"You can do a lot of things for me, but right now I have to use the phone to call for a taxi." Jason softly chuckled.

"I can give you a ride to wherever ever you are going," Rita said with a smile.

"Thank you. However, I don't have high confidence in woman drivers," joked Jason with a laugh. Jason called for a taxi. Once the taxi appeared and parked in Rita's driveway, Jason said bye to Rita. On his way out the door, Jason reminded Rita regarding the date they had the day after. Jason got into the taxi and gave the driver the address of the motel where he was staying. Comfortably seated and relaxed in the back seat, he kept wondering where Cyrus had gone to.

Jason was fearful that Cyrus perhaps would be following him. Almost three miles away from the motel Jason asked to the taxi driver to stop short of the destination. After he paid the taxi driver, Jason walked the rest of the way to the motel. He was very concerned that if Cyrus discovered where he was staying, Cyrus would do harm or perhaps would kill Jason. He sensed that Cyrus was not an intelligent man, but he was a diabolical person, and he would do anything to take all of Jason's money. It was a long walk for Jason. He wasn't relaxing. Every small number of steps he took, he kept looking at the back of him, hoping to confirm that Cyrus wasn't following him. He walked his way to the motel through the back streets and the alleys. He made numerous stops to make sure that he wasn't followed.

Finally, he arrived at the motel. As soon as he walked in, he asked the employee if anyone came looking for him. The desk clerk told Jason that no one came. Jason opened the door to his room; he sat down and began to think whether he ought to stay there or to find somewhere else to stay. Promptly, he got up and started packing his clothes. He waited until it got dark. He crawled out from the bathroom window and walked towards the nearest phone booth, and then he called for a taxi.

When the taxi arrived, he hurriedly opened the back door and threw his clothes on the back seat, and he got in as fast as he could. Jason didn't want to look suspicious, and he joked with the driver, "Damn wife. I just cannot make her content. No matter what I do for her; she is never quite satisfied," Jason commented. The driver looked back threw the rear-view mirror and asked Jason if he had been kicked out of the house.

Jason wanted to keep the conversation going, told the driver, "Yup, my house, and I have to leave." Jason asked the taxi driver to take him to an uptown hotel.

He wanted to be closer to Rita's house. The day after, Jason woke up early. He well remembered the get-together he promised Rita; he took a shower and got dressed. After he was done, he called for a taxi to take him to Rita's house. Jason was nervous about Cyrus that he might be still looking for him. At around twenty minutes to ten, Jason was on Rita's door step. Anxiously, she couldn't wait for Jason to get there. Almost immediately, she saw Jason getting out of the taxi; she ran to the door and opened it without giving Jason any time for him to knock on the door.

Chapter 13
The Luncheon

Jason approached Rita and said to her, "Well, good morning. I hope that I am not late?"

"Good morning to you. You look very attractive in that outfit," Rita casually remarked. She asked Jason if he had a notion where they were going for lunch. Jason responded that they could determine the place while they were driving around.

They walked toward Rita's car. "Since you don't have confidence in women drivers, then you drive and look for a place where we can have a nice luncheon," Rita told Jason, and she passed the car keys to Jason.

Jason looked at the keys smiled and said, "I was only joking when I said that to you. I haven't driven a car for a long time. I can't remember the last time that I drove." With a gloomy look on his face; Jason handed the car keys back to Rita, smiled, and got in the car. "Well, where are we going?" he asked.

"Don't worry. I know a good and quiet restaurant where we can eat and have a peaceful conversation," Rita answered as she drove away. On their course to the restaurant, they talked about the treasure and the trip.

Rita told Jason how nervous she was to sail all the way to Europe, given that she had never been on a boat previously. She showed her cheerfulness to spend time with her dad. When Jason asked her how she sensed about Samantha and Cyrus, Rita got too disturbed because of what she experienced in the past week. Rita stopped the car in front of a restaurant; they walked inside. Rita pointed toward a table in the back of the room by the window. Jason pulled a chair out for Rita to sit on. His hands were shaking; he wasn't relaxed at all. Unexpectedly, Jason didn't feel to mingle; he desired to eat and get out of the restaurant. Cyrus was on his mind. He was suspicious Rita, by her charming personality, was doing undercover work for Cyrus. There weren't many detailed discussions between Rita and Jason during their first luncheon together. Rita actually observed the unforeseen changes in Jason, and she was mainly concerned about Jason's conduct. After they completed eating Jason paid the head waiter, and they walked back to the car.

Driving back to Rita's house Jason kept extremely silent. He commenced to have fondness towards Rita, but he wasn't sure if he could have great loyalty in her. Jason was trying hard to keep his affection towards Rita under control because he didn't want to obstruct his mental state of mind. He had to be ready to act, especially if Cyrus tried to take revenge for what Jason did to him to humiliate him. Rita kept looking at Jason because of his silence since they left the restaurant, and she wanted to break the stillness and asked Jason why he was so relatively quiet. He looked at her and said, "I just can't vaguely remember the last time I went out on a date." He replied with a grin on his face. The thoughts about his past filled his heart with sadness. They arrived at the house; Rita parked the car and asked Jason to go in. Jason got uneasy and created an excuse that he had plans for that afternoon.

Rita was saddened with Jason's response because she had her own plans for Jason.

"Oh, by the way, my dad requires you to come over on Saturday to verify the supplies that you ask for. He needs you to make certain that he got everything you required," Rita said. Jason inquired the time that Richard wished to meet with him on his yacht.

"He didn't tell me. Give me a phone call and we can make arrangements to pick you up," Rita replied.

Jason started walking off without comprehending that he was miles far from his motel where he was staying. Walking was no problem for him; after all, that is what he had done for these last twelve years. He was thinking about Rita, and he was speculative if she was sincere, or was she trying to use her tenderness to ambush him? Perhaps Richard is utilizing her to attempt to find a way to get the information from Jason regarding the treasure and that's why she is so affectionate toward him. "Just can't trust anybody when it comes to money," Jason said to himself while he was on his way to the hotel.

Saturday morning, Jason phoned Rita to exactly determine the time Richard wanted to meet with him. Rita told him that the sooner the better, because Richard had to meet some of his old friends. Jason gave her the localities where he would be waiting for her.

Rita got prepared to get together with Jason once again and hoping that this time Jason would be more socialized with her. She was highly excited also because she was going to visit for the first time in her life her father's yacht. She rushed into the house and drove away to meet up with Jason.

Jason was waiting for Rita at the site where he told her to pick him up. As soon as she arrived, Jason got into the car, and they said hello to each other, the same as Rita drove away to the marina where Richard's yacht was anchored. Jason was more at ease than the previous day they met; he was more conversational. He promised to himself not to demonstrate that he didn't have confidence in anyone, including Rita. They arrived at the marina; Jason and Rita were astonished when they saw Richards's yacht. "I am impressed with your dad's toy," he exclaimed and continued to speak how huge and luxurious that the yacht was.

Richard was waiting anxiously on board, and saw Jason and Rita walking towards the yacht. He was perfectly content as soon as he had seen Rita and Jason together. He called their names and waved at them. "Come aboard!" he shouted.

Rita was absolutely amazed with her father's yacht, particularly because she never saw her father's yacht, notably when she closely observed her dad was in high spirits. She ran up the steps, and hugged her father. "Oh Dad, this is gorgeous, and it is so big," Rita said with an enjoyable look on her face.

"Thank you, my dear, and welcome on board," Richard replied cheerfully.

Jason took his time getting to embark. He looked around and didn't see Cyrus, wondering where Cyrus had been.

"Good morning, Jason," Richard said. "Welcome on board. We got the supplies; I would like you to look over to make sure that we got everything that we especially need. We don't want to forget anything now, do we?" Richard comically commented.

"We are going to need everything that I had written down," Jason replied.

Richard led the way to the storeroom with Jason and Rita following him. "There is everything you asked for. I bought double of everything to make sure that nothing goes wrong," Richard said.

Jason was astonished when he saw the amount of the supplies and asked, "Why did you double on everything?"

"You never know. I wanted to make sure that we are well fully equipped," Richard replied.

Richard handed over the supply list that Jason gave him and said, "Here, check it out. Make sure that we did not forget to buy anything. Are you sure this is all we need?" he asked.

"I think that you got more than what we require," Jason replied with an overwhelmed look. Jason marked off from the list every item as he carefully inspected the supplies piece by piece. "The whole thing seems to be in order," Jason replied as he shrugged his shoulders.

"Good, let me show you kids around." Richard took Jason and Rita for a tour of the yacht; and also introduced them to the crew members.

"What time are we going to have lunch?" Richard asked the chef. The chef informed Richard that he will serve lunch in half an hour.

"Let's go and have a drink while we wait to eat," Richard suggested.

Jason was more nervous than ever before; he did not see Cyrus.

Rita and Richard kept talking about the trip, and Jason remained actively sitting silently. "What is the matter, Jason? Why are you are so hushed?" Richard asked as he noted that Jason was not participating in their discussion.

"Nothing, I am just like that. I do not like to rudely interrupt; besides, you two have a lot of catching to do. My job is to guide you to find the Maltese Falcon, the golden bird. I am not here to socialize." Jason rose up and walked towards the bar.

He poured himself second drink, turned around facing Richard and said, "All I care is that you pay me the other half of the money after we come up with the Falcon. That's the deal." And he walked away.

Richard did not know what to say to Jason and looked at Rita, surprised with Jason's performance. He asked Rita if there was something annoying Jason. She told him about the night before when they went for dinner and how Jason appeared very mysterious. The waiter approached Richard and told him that lunch was ready to be served, asked Richard where he would prefer to eat lunch. Richard, who was still a little stunned by Jason's unusual manners, told the waiter that he could serve lunch on deck.

Meanwhile, Jason was thinking if this may perhaps be a setup by the four of them to prematurely terminate him after he leads them to the cave. Jason nervously leaned on the railing, he kept wondering where Cyrus was. He watched Richard and Rita during their conversation and noticed that when he looked at them, they stopped talking to each other.

Rita called Jason to join them for lunch; he gradually walked near the dinner table, sat down, and he commenced to eat. The three of them did not say a word to each throughout lunch.

After they finished eating Jason broke the silence and asked Richard, "When can we leave? Are Cyrus and Samantha coming along? By the way, where are Cyrus and Sam?" Jason asked apprehensively because he could no longer anticipate. He had to ask because he was getting nervous not knowing where Cyrus was.

"Oh, Samantha required buying some new garments for the trip; Cyrus is driving her around. And, to answer your question, we can leave for Malta on Monday. It is that satisfactory to you?" Richard replied.

"Okay," Rita said while she bounced up and down.

"Why don't you cease acting like a child," Jason told her, as he stood up and asked, "What time should I be here on Monday?"

"What is it with you? Why are you so miserable?" Rita asked nervously. She could not quite understand why Jason was behaving so rudely.

Richard calmly replied, "Anytime, the sooner the better."

"That's fine. I will see on Monday morning then. I'll be here early," Jason said and headed toward the steps to leave.

"Wait. Where are you going?" Rita asked as she strolled towards Jason.

Rudely, Jason asked, "I beg your pardon?"

"I mean, don't you need a ride back?" she asked with a slightly confused look on her face.

Jason continued to walk down the steps and told Rita that he would prefer to walk and want to be left alone. Richard and Rita looked at each other astonished. "What is wrong with him? Is he going crazy?" Richard asked. He was on the edge to lose his patient.

"I don't know, perhaps returning back to Malta is bringing him bad childhood memories," Rita replied. "Dad, it was nice to see you again. I have some shopping to do myself before Monday." Rita gave her dad a kiss and ran towards the ramp.

"Rita, I have something to say to you," Richard shouted.

Rita stopped in the middle of the ramp and wondered what her dad wanted to say to her. Richard stepped towards Rita and asked her to get back on the yacht. Rita told him that she could not, and she had to go.

Richard stepped closer to Rita, and softly he told her, "You don't need to rush; Jason couldn't have gotten too far." Richard smiled.

Rita looked at her father and said, "I don't understand, what do you mean?"

"Listen, I know I haven't been a good parent, but I don't like seeing you getting hurt. I see the way you look at him. The same look that your mother used to give me. Be cautious; don't rush him," Richard softly said while Rita looked at her dad in tears.

Chapter 14
Falling In Love

"Oh, Dad, he is so completely honest and affectionate. I have to find him."
Rita ran as fast as she could to her car. She jumped in her car and sped away
eagerly so she could catch up with Jason.

She kept looking around at the same time she was driving, and instantly
she saw Jason sitting comfortable at an outdoor bar. She parked the car at
the back of the bar, walked slowly behind Jason, and asked, "Where do you
have to go in such urgency?"

Jason looked back and said, "What are you doing here? Are you spying
on me?" he asked with rather insensitive voice.

Rita inquired if she could sit down and Jason, still furious replied, "Go
ahead, it's a free country."

"What is wrong with you? Why you have been acting like an uncivilized
man?" Rita asked.

Calmly, Jason said, "You definitely desire to know? I will tell you, it is
you. I do not know if I can trust you. I have been unaccompanied for over
twelve years, with no money and no place to sleep and no one gave a care
about me. Now you come along, and you want to be my best pal. Why, Rita?
You can tell your dad that I will not betray him. I don't very much appreci-
ate being questioned, what, where, and when, nobody gives a shit about a
homeless person. Now I have to answer to your dad, worry about the other

asshole, Cyrus; everything is happening so fast. I just do not know what to do anymore. I wish that I never found that stupid newspaper. You are the sole one that is being respectable to me. Why? What are you trying to do?" He was very somewhat annoyed because he did not trust her except he had mixed emotions towards her. Jason wondered whose side she was taking.

"Do you want to talk about it?" Rita asked as she touched his face.

Jason pushed her hand aside from his face and said, "Look, sister, why don't you leave me alone? All you care is that I don't run away and steal your father's treasure," Jason told her.

"You are mistaken, Jason. We do trust you, and you have proven to us when you came back. I like you, Jason, and I have not at any time met a man before like you, so truly honest and pretty sensitive. I will tell you something personal, I have never been on a date in my life. I was terrified to fall in love with somebody after what transpired to my parents. You are the first one that I had any emotion towards," Rita told Jason as tears ran down her face.

Jason felt deeply embarrassed, because he had no idea that Rita was serious about starting a relationship with him. He didn't want to show his soft side of him; especially the way he treated Rita. "Fall in love? What is that?" smiled Jason while he took Rita's hand and gently squeezed it in his hand.

"Listen, I am fond of you too and we both had bad experiences in our lives. Let's take it easy; moreover, we have to focus on the treasure hunt, and once that is over. I will steal you from your dad." They both stood up and hugged.

He still didn't have total trust in Rita; he asked her to drive him to the same location where she had picked him up early that morning. They arrived at the destination; Jason stepped out of the car and asked Rita if she could pick him up on Monday. "Of course," she replied. She asked for the location where she could pick up Jason.

He told her that he would call her on Monday morning at seven o'clock, and he would inform her.

Rita drove away wondering why Jason would not tell her where he was staying.

Perhaps he has his individual plans for the treasure, and that he is going to use her for his self-intention. She was not so sure if she ought to trust

Jason and kept thinking about Jason's comments when he said, "We have to focus on the treasure hunt."

Chapter 15
The Voyage

Back on the *Slik*, Richard was absolutely ecstatic about the voyage, in particular, sailing to an island that he had never visited. Down in his cabin, Richard and the captain were going through the navigation charts as they carefully planned for the expedition to Malta. Cyrus and Samantha arrived at the yacht after they ended her shopping; Cyrus asked a crewman where Richard was. The crewman replied to Cyrus that Richard was in his cabin with the captain.

Cyrus walked with Samantha into her cabin and softly whispered to her, "Pretty soon we will be rich." He kissed Samantha.

"I can't understand you, Cyrus. What is going on? What sort of a plan do you have?" Samantha asked Cyrus.

"Don't be largely concerned, you will see; I'll teach them both a lesson." Cyrus kissed Samantha and left towards his cabin.

When Richard and the Captain accurately completed the charting, Richard went immediately to Cyrus's cabin. He knocked on the cabin door; Cyrus opened the door and asked Richard to step in. Richard unhurriedly stepped inside and informed Cyrus that they would be sailing to Malta on Monday morning.

"Did you tell that bum?" And was everything he arranged us to purchase is in order?" sarcastically Cyrus asked.

Richard calmly looked at Cyrus; he put his right hand on Cyrus's shoulder and said, "Cyrus, I have known you for a long time. Listen to me; if you start any trouble with Jason, I swear I'll be forced to kill you," Richard warned Cyrus. He grabbed Cyrus by the throat and shoved him against the cabin door. Richard walked out of the cabin and slammed the door behind him. "Maybe I will kill you first," Cyrus angrily whispered to himself knowing Richard had left and could not hear him. Samantha heard the uproar and went to Cyrus's cabin.

When she entered the cabin, she looked at Cyrus's face; she immediately recognized that he was very angry. "I'll kill them all. You and I will experience how rich people live. This yacht and the golden bird will be ours," Cyrus told Samantha. Cyrus was very upset. Samantha tried to cool his temper down; she started to flourish with Cyrus's groin.

Monday arrived rapidly for Jason; he had an emotionally disturbed night. He kept thinking about his family, and his friends that he left behind in Malta. After twelve years of being away from his homeland, he was going back. He finished packing for the voyage, and he sat down on the edge of his bed. Too many thoughts were going through his head as he picked up the phone and called Rita to pick him up from the hotel. It was not long after he had called Rita was outside the hotel waiting for him. This time Jason gave Rita the address of the hotel where he was staying at. Jason got in the car and looked at Rita and told her that she looked a bit tired. She told him that she had a tough time sleeping because of all the excitement. When they arrived at the yachting marina, Richard and the crew were waiting for them to start the long-anticipated journey, sailing to Malta.

Cyrus was currently waiting at the bottom of the ramp for them to greed them. Jason and Rita walked towards him, and Cyrus asked one of the crew members to take their luggage on board the yacht and to take them into their cabins.

To Jason's big surprise, Cyrus handed a handshake, and he escorted them on board. Richard was watching from the upper deck, and he was completely stunned to see Cyrus's friendly gesture towards Jason. Cyrus took Jason to his cabin and asked if they could be friends. "Let's forget about the past and let's start a new friendship," Cyrus said as he put his hand out to shake it with Jason.

Jason smiled and said, "Cyrus, I would love that," and they both shook hands. However, deep down, inside, they both knew that they secretly despised each other and that there would be no trusting each other.

During the voyage, Jason and Cyrus became good associates, at least it seemed like that to Richard and Rita. They drank jointly and had lots of fun to Richard's pleasant surprise. Samantha also eventually became friends with Rita and the five of them became like one happy family. They have been sailing for almost five weeks. The yacht captain informed Richard that they would be arriving in Malta approximately in twelve hours. As a result of the news Richard excited rushed to the sitting area where Jason, Rita, Cyrus, and Samantha were sitting telling jokes.

"The Captain just informed me that we will be in Malta in about twelve hours," Richard told them.

"Finally, I can't wait until I walk on firm ground," Samantha said as she snuggled with Richard. Rita looked at Jason and said to him that he would be home soon.

"That's nice," Jason replied. He got up from his chair with an unhappy look on his face and headed towards the railing.

"What's wrong with him? He should be happy, not sad," Cyrus commented.

"It's a long story. Don't worry about him. I'll go have a talk with him," Rita said as she walked towards Jason. When she got close to Jason, she noticed that he had tears coming down his face as he was fixedly staring at the waves.

"What's wrong? You do not seem too very joyful. You should be, you are just about home. I can't visualize how hard this has been for you," Rita said to Jason, as she put her arms around him. Jason did not say a word; he just stood gazing at the waves.

Rita knew what was disturbing Jason, and she stood looking at the distant horizon. "This is beautiful blue water. I have never seen anything like this before," Rita said, trying to get Jason to talk.

"Yes, it is, and it will get even nicer," Jason replied as he kept staring down at the waves.

"Are you going to look for them?" smoothly, Rita asked.

"Look for whom?" questioned Jason.

"Your family," Rita replied.

"I have been dead for twelve years to them. You don't understand," Jason replied.

"Then, why are you so sad if you have no intentions to look for them?" Rita asked.

"You know what?" Jason said as he turned to face Rita. "You inquire lots of hypothetical questions, and I am telling you for the last time, I never want to talk about my past again. Stop acting as if you were my mother."

He removed Rita's hand from around him and walked towards the bar and ordered a glass of rum.

"What the hell are you all looking at?" Jason yelled back in an angry voice as he looked straight at the four of them. They could see the rage in Jason's eyes. Rita had no nerve to look at Jason; she knew what he had been going throughout his life. She felt the same way Jason was feeling for a long time until she met him.

She knew the deep sorrows that Jason was going through. She grew up basically deprived of parents, granted that the death of her mother and her father was not at any time around her, now unhappiness came upon her once again.

Rita, with a teary eye, slowly walked towards Jason and modestly said, "I am sorry, Jason. It will not happen again." Rita strolled away and left to her cabin. Richard, Cyrus, and Samantha went down to Rita's cabin to confer her. Jason felt awful and dishonourable for the way he angrily responded. He knew he should not have yelled at Rita, after all she is trying to strongly encourage him to connect with his family once again. In anger, he threw the glass that he had in his hand in the sea. He walked to the stern side looked at the horizon, and he could see the island of Malta in the far distance. Jason quickly proceeded down below looking for Richard and told him that they were almost in Malta.

Richard looked through the window, he turned around, and with an angry look on his face and told Jason that he had no explanation to behave in the manner that he did towards Rita. "She is my daughter, and no one unfairly treats her like that, especially you. What is wrong with you? Are you blind?" Richard asked. "She likes you, asshole. She thinks that you are the best thing that ever happened to her. You surely don't deserve her. You and I, it's business, once our business is done, I'll pay you the rest of the money and leave. I don't want to see or hear from you ever again, and I'll suggest you to leave Rita alone, if you know what's good for you." Jason walked out of Richard's cabin, very humiliated.

On his way out, he bumped into Samantha as she was entering Richard's cabin. "We are there, babe. We are in Malta," Richard said as he smiled.

Cyrus walked into Richard's cabin to notify him that they are finally arriving at land. He looked at Samantha and winked at her, and pointed to the door.

Cyrus walked out and soon after Samantha followed. She headed toward the hallway where Cyrus was waiting for her. "What do you want?" Samantha asked anxiously.

"Listen, from this day forwards, you do what I tell you. Do not ask at all any questions and perform normal. Just be you and everything will turn out perfectly satisfactory for us," Cyrus told her.

"Okay, but don't push your luck," Samantha replied, as they went on deck to join the others.

Rita leaned over the side of the yacht and yelled, "There is a coast guard boat heading our way."

The captain came down on deck and told everyone to have their passports ready because the customs officers were coming aboard. "We haven't even docked yet," Richard exclaimed.

"I guess they function in a different structure in this country," the captain replied.

Chapter 16
Return to Malta

The coast guard boat pulled over against the *Slik* and two of the customs officers got on board the yacht. They went through the procedure of checking everyone on board the yacht.

"Everything seems to be in order," said one of the customs officers. The other officers commented to Richard that they traveled a long way. The other customs officer asked the captain what was the purpose of them to be in Malta. The captain, not very well knowing anything why Richard sailed to Malta, told the officer that he worked for Richard and that his boss likes to travel around the world. While the customs officers were talking to the captain, Jason softly whispered to Richard that if the customs officers ask him what they are doing in Malta, to simply tell them that they were there for a vacation.

The customs officers came down on the deck and asked to speak to Richard.

"Yes, what can I do for you? I hope that you found our legal documents in order?" Richard asked.

"Yes, sir, everything is in order, but I have to ask you some questions," the officer replied. Richard got a little nervous because he was afraid that they were going to ask him about the provisions that they stored away.

"Sure," replied Richard.

The officer continued with the questioning. "We noticed that you are carrying a huge amount of extraordinary of supplies, why and for what use? My other question is what is the purpose behind the visit to Malta? And how long are you planning on staying?" asked the officer as he looked around the deck and noticed that the other four passengers were sitting silently at the bar.

"We are here on vacation. You see, my daughter is going to marry that guy over there," as he pointed toward Jason. "His name is Jason; he is Maltese, so we came to Malta to meet his family before they get married. We are planning on staying in Malta for approximately six weeks. Jason told us that you had plenty of beautiful fiestas in Malta."

"That is so wonderful, romantic. Yes, we do have many fiestas in Malta. I am pretty sure that you will enjoy them. Good luck and have a nice stay," the customs officer replied.

The officers climbed downward to board their boat. Halfway down, one of the officers got back up on the *Slik* and asked Richard when the wedding was going to take place. Nervously, Richard replied that no date had been set yet and that once he meets Jason's family then they will decide upon a date. The officer saluted to Richard and boarded the boat.

"What the hell is going on?" Jason asked in a mad voice. "Why did you say that to them? Suppose they asked you where my family lives? You're an idiot."

"Calm down, Jason, that is all I could come up with. It was a good excuse, too. They didn't ask again about the supplies," laughed Richard. Jason was very upset and left in a rush to his cabin.

"Dad, you know how sensitive he is about family relationships. Why did you say that? He told you to tell them that we were on vacation. You make me sick," Rita said as she walked away.

Escorted by the coast guard boat, the *Slik* pulled into the harbour.

The captain followed the navigation chart that the customs officer gave him to where he would anchor. Once they docked at the marina, Richard gave his crew three weeks holiday to enjoy themselves. Soon the crew left the yacht, Richard told Rita to tell Jason that he wanted to have a brief discussion with him in Richard's cabin.

Rita nervously went to Jason's cabin and told him that her dad wanted to meet with him. Jason walked into Richards's cabin, and Richard told Jason to sit and not to interrupt.

"Jason, I know we have our major differences between us, but now I want to let you know that I am putting you in full command of this search. You know this island more than us and, feasibly, you speak Maltese. As I have already told you, once we find the treasure, our joint venture ends. I will have the rest of the money with me, all you have to do is to bring to me the Maltese Falcon, and you will receive the rest of the reward money. Anyway, you are the man solely responsible now."

Jason was in a state of surprise. He never expected to hear anything like that from Richard. He told Richard that he was aware of his duties, and he has respect for his employer.

Jason promised Richard that he would do everything that he can to recover the Maltese Falcon for him. Jason thanked Richard for putting his trust in him, and then he asked Richard if he had told Cyrus yet. Richard told Jason that he had already discussed this matter at length with Cyrus and that Cyrus had approved of Richard's choice for Jason to direct the exploration.

"When are you going to start?" Richard asked.

"The first basic thing that I have to do is to establish the area where the cave is. I will take Rita with me, and we have to make it look as we are sightseeing."

"All of us have to be extra careful whom we talk to and what we say. Mainly, what we are doing is stealing something that belongs to the people on this island. If we are captured, we will all end up in jail for the rest of our lives. Once I locate the cave, then I will let everyone know when the search begins." Jason told Richard that the day after he took Rita with him to locate the cave and at the same time, she could enjoy viewing the historic sites.

Rita was on her way to her dad's cabin when she overheard the conversation between Jason and her dad. Slowly, she walked in and said, "I'm sure that I will enjoy the tour, especially when the tour guide is you." Rita was joyful to hear that from Jason, but one thing was bothering her: why the sudden change In Jason's behaviour? Is he going to use her to blackmail her dad or possibly harm her?

"We have to rent a car. So, come on let's go," Jason said and grabbed Rita's hand and pull her out from the cabin as they ran up the stairs much amused.

Richard was cheerful when he saw Rita and Jason behaving like little kids. He stepped out from the cabin door and yelled at Jason. "You take good care of my daughter!"

Jason yelled back. "Don't worry, I will." Richard disoriented about what at this moment happened and mumble to himself, "Go figure, and I told him to stay away from her."

Rita and Jason went ashore and called for a taxi to take them to a car rental garage.

When they entered the rental garage, Jason asked for the manager as he spoke in Maltese. He was directed to the manager's office by one of the workers; Jason introduced Rita and himself to the manager. Since Jason had no driving license, he bribed the manger by giving some money so he could rent the car. When they got to the car, Rita told Jason that she was greatly surprised to hear him speak Maltese. Rita was pretty excited, and she asked Jason if she could drive. Jason strongly reminded her that, in Malta, they drive on the left side of the road, and to be an extra careful driver since few drivers in Malta follow the street law. Jason did not mind, and he let her do the driving and told Rita to stop at the first souvenir shop to buy a map of the island. Nearby Jason spotted a souvenir shop and told Rita to pull over.

Jason went inside the shop and purchased a map. Jason examined the map and routed the location they had to go. It did not take them long to reach the location.

"Where are we?" Rita asked anxiously. Jason told her that in English, the area was called Zurrieq Valley. Jason carefully looked around and could not be fully acquainted with the area; he had been away too long. Jason asked one of the locals where they could get a boat to tour the area. They were directed to follow the road down the hill.

They walked down the hill; Rita looked around and she was astonished. Rita asked Jason why the tiny harbour was full of boats. He told her that most of those boats were fishing boats, and some of them were touring boats.

Chapter 17
The Search Begins

They finally reached the bottom of the hill when one of the tour guides asked them if they required a boat tour. Jason replied yes, and they were led to one of the tour boats.

"You wait here until more people come," said the tour guide with broken English. Jason tried clearly to explain to the guide that they wanted the tour for just the two of them. Jason didn't speak Maltese to the tour guide because he didn't want the tour guide to be rather suspicious.

"More money for two only," quickly replied the guide.

Jason looked at Rita and told that Malta had changed a lot but not the people. "Okay, here is more money." Jason pulled out extra cash and gave it to the guide. The tour guide grabbed the money and told them to get in the boat.

Jason and Rita stepped carefully into the boat as Jason slowly opened one of the treasure maps that he had borrowed from Richard, while Rita got the camera ready to take pictures of the beautiful surroundings. The tour guide kept looking at Jason's map since it looked totally different. The tour is commonly known as the Blue Grotto tour. A tour guide would take visitors in and out of various caves and have a beautiful view of the deep, clear blue water. Jason told Rita to watch closely for a cave within a cave as he tried to compare the location on the map.

"This is the most remarkably beautiful blue water I have ever seen," Rita said as she reached out to the side of the boat and put the palm of her hand into the water.

The tour took them to various caves, and Jason started to get worried. "How many more caves are there?" Jason asked, anticipating.

The tour guide told Jason that there were about four caves left, and the big cave named the Blue Grotto means the blue cave.

They proceeded into the next cave, as the boat was slowly circling around to get out, Jason told the tour guide to slow down and to circle back to the end of the cave to get a closer look to what appeared to be another cave opening. The guide circled the boat towards the area that Jason was pointing at. The guide firmly told Jason that the boat could not enter the other cave since the opening of the cave entrance is slightly too small for the boat to enter.

Jason told the guide to stop as he took a good photo of the cave.

"That's it. Look, the letter 'H' is engraved on top of the small entrance," Rita exclaimed.

"Oh yeah. I was right, let's go back," Jason told the tour guide to carry on with the tour. Jason asked Rita to take several photographs of the locality and of the cave entrance.

Both were tremendously excited; Jason placed his arms around Rita's shoulder and told her, "I told you that I would find it."

Rita was very excited, and her legs were shaking uncontrollably, such that Jason had to tell her to relax before she tipped the boat over.

"I can't. I am so absolutely thrilled yet I am so nervous," Rita acknowledged as she clutched Jason's hand and squeezed hard. Jason was further excited than Rita, but he kept perfectly tranquil. Now he could not wait to get his vengeance.

Back on land, Rita asked Jason, "I don't fully understand. The map shows that the other cave is above the sea level and the entire caves that we toured are all at water level."

"That cave access leads us to the main cave entrance. Look at this," as he pointed to the map. "Once we get into the small cave entrance then we have to find the other entrance that will take us to these passages." Jason tried to explain in detail as he pointed at the map.

Rita had a hard time to comprehend what Jason was trying desperately to explain to her. She immediately started to wonder about the very unexpected change of Jason's conduct. Rita got numb when she thought that Jason would do harm to Richard, Cyrus and Samantha; what about her? Would he harm her? Rita was apprehensive; she lost her footing going up the hill and fell down. Jason helped her up, and with a smile on his face asked her if she was all right. "I can't figure this out," Rita commented.

"Don't worry, I know what I am doing," Jason replied. "Let's go back to the marina, and give Richard the good news. We have a lot of work and planning to do."

Slowly, they made it to car; Jason got behind the driving wheel and told Rita that he was going to take the lengthy way to the marina, so he'd be able to show her some of the aged structures and the Spanish forts.

Rita panicked and pondered why Jason was taking the long way back to the marina, and if he was using excuses for his aim to harm her.

Jason was driving exceptionally cautiously; most of the streets in Malta were fairly narrow, and in addition he had not driven a car for over twelve years. Jason took Rita to various memorable sites, and he had a history of every site that they visited.

Rita became, to some extent, relaxed because Jason did what he had told her he would: show her around the historic sites.

On the yacht, Richard was waiting impatiently and wondering why it was taking Jason hours to return. Richard had full confidence in Jason, but there was a considerable amount of money involved; if Jason could get to the Maltese Falcon on his own, he would make millions of dollars. Perhaps Jason used Rita as the lure to get to the Falcon, and then he would terminate her. Too many concepts were going through Richard's head. It began to get dark and Richard, from the upper deck where he was sitting quietly, saw Jason and Rita parking the car. He became comforted, got up, and ran to the railing, to wait for them. He didn't give them time to get on board; as soon as they were close to him, he yelled at them if they had successfully found the place. Jason and Rita boarded the yacht. Jason told Richard that, indeed, they definitely found the first cave entrance. Richard, eyes wide open, asked where the Falcon was.

"No, you fool, we only found the main entrance," exclaimed Jason. Cyrus was sitting around the bar, over heard the conversation, stood up and walked towards Jason, looked at him and kept walking. Cyrus leant against the railing, spat into the water and mumbled to himself, "I am going to be rich and the bum is going to help me come to be one."

Jason opened the map to demonstrate to Richard, "This is the main cave entrance. As you see the letter 'H' is engraved on top of the second cave entrance, this is where we have to start. Once we get in, we have to find the other cave entrance that will lead us to these passages. This passageway is the only way into the big cave. Protecting the cave, there will be a massive cliff encircling the cave. This is why no person ever found Hassan's cave. The cliffs completely conceal the entrance to the cave where the treasure is." Jason got interrupted by Cyrus and pointed out the third map which showed that the big cave was enclosed by water. He wanted to know how they were going to get inside the cave where the treasure was. Jason explained that they would need the rubber dinghy, and they would have to look around for the cave that is above the water level. "According to the stories, the cave is about three to four hundred feet above the water level. We will have to climb up to the cave, and the quest begins," finished Jason.

"Why can't we use the *Slik* rather than the rubber dinghy?" Cyrus inquired further.

"Because of the cliff surrounding the inner cave and there is no other way in. The only time that we can use the *Slik* is to take us to the entrance where Rita and I visited. Richard will have to wait on the yacht for us," Jason replied.

"Wait a minute. You mean to tell me that I don't get to participate in the search? How are we supposed to get to this cave if it is concealed behind this huge cliff?" he asked.

Jason told everybody that it wouldn't be an easy task, and they have to make sure that they have all the necessities with them.

He specifically instructed them that besides the equipment, they have to take bottled water with them because he was sure that it would be very hot inside the narrow passages. Samantha asked if she could also be involved in the search.

Jason strongly reminded everybody that only Richard stays behind, and he has to be ready to pick them up once they return with the Maltese Falcon.

It appeared that none of them could identify with what Jason was trying to say. Rita got doubtful of what Jason told them about the search; on the other hand, Cyrus was taking everything that Jason was saying with concentration; after all, he had his own plans also. Richard didn't worry not to involve himself in the search; after all, he had been completely trustworthy in Jason. All of them appeared puzzled, and after a moment of hush Cyrus broke the silence and asked, "So, when do we start?"

Jason replied that the search would start the day after and declared them to be prepared and to wear light clothing, since once they were in the tunnels it would be exceptionally hot. "Have a good night's sleep. You are going to need it," Jason finished saying, as he rolled the map and walked toward his cabin.

Jason was awake early the next morning. He got up on deck with a cup of coffee in his hand as he watched the sun rising from the horizon. He double-checked the gear that they would need and organized everything. Jason guided Richard to the whereabouts on the map they would have to sail to get started.

Richard cruised to where Jason had indicated to him. Before long, they finally arrived to the cave entrance. Cyrus got increasingly alarmed when he saw a large number of small boats going in and out of the dock and asked, "Why are all these boats out here?" Rita explained to him that they were touring boats that take the tourists to the caves. Cyrus was not comfortable with that situation; he had to make entirely different plans for his scheme. Once they reached the location outside the entrance to the cave, Richard anchored the yacht.

Chapter 18
Inside The Cave

Jason organized the equipment and told everyone to start loading them in the two dinghies. Cyrus and Jason took the first trip to the cave and drop off the supplies; Rita and Samantha followed after. Jason returned to the yacht and told Richard that if someone asked him what they are doing just to tell them that they are shooting a movie. Jason instructed Richard to stay close by and not to wander around the area.

"Where do you expect me to go? I am not leaving this area until you guys return with my Falcon," Richard replied. Cyrus left the girls at the cave entrance and went back to the yacht to help Jason unload the remaining supplies.

Jason passed down to Cyrus a whale harpoon. "What do we need this huge harpoon for?" Cyrus asked.

"Do you know a better way to throw a rope four hundred feet up to reach the upper cave entrance?" Jason questioned.

Cyrus did not say a word to Jason; besides, he had other plans to make use of the harpoon. Both headed back to the cave where they had left Rita and Samantha waiting eagerly. The four of them, one by one crawled through the small cave entrance that led them to a larger cave, dragging behind them the supplies. "Now everyone has to stay close to each other and to extend the use of the batteries; we'll use two flashlights, one in the front, and one at the back," Jason instructed them.

Once they came in, the main cave got completely dark and incredibly hot just like Jason told them. Jason lead the way entering the passage, the others followed.

Some of the winding passages were so narrow that they had to crawl upon their hands and knees to go through, hauling the bags with the supplies. Over two hours went by and there was no sign at the end to the passage. Everybody was perspiring but no one hence had complained of the difficult conditions. Inside the passageway was pitch dark and slightly damp; water was dribbling from just about all over the passage, making the walkway very slippery.

The narrow passage made it very difficult to move around, especially with the supplies they were carrying. Rita was the first that asked for a rest and questioned Jason. "Are you sure we are going the right way?" Jason told her that was the only way in and out to the cave. Samantha initially began to bitterly complain that she was getting tired; they rested for a while, and then they continued. With Jason leading the way, he kept encouraging the others not to stop when unexpectedly he stopped. "Listen to that. Can you hear the sound from the waves?"

Every one of them got silenced and Cyrus from the back yelled, "I can't hear anything."

Jason was sure of what he heard and continued leading the way.

Jason kept encouraging the others and shouted out that they must be getting closer. He stopped again. "Listen to the waves," he loudly exclaimed. The others heard the sound from the waves also. They could feel a gentle cool breeze approach towards them. Jason yelled out that he was actually seeing sunlight, in the distance. The closer they got, the brighter the inside the passage became, and finally, "Here we are," said Jason as dropped down to his knees, took off his backpack and jumped into the water.

"You are right. I wonder why nobody ever found this place," Rita whispered.

Jason was tremendously enjoying the cool water said to Rita, "One man did, and that was Hassan."

Jason sat down on the warm sand, and the others ran into the water to refreshingly cool off. It was getting close to sundown, Jason told the other three that they had to make camp for the night, and they will continue the search in the morning.

The three of them fully agreed, and they got something to eat. Once they finished eating, each one of them opened their sleeping bags and tried to get comfortable to get some sleep. They were very tired out from the hiking inside the hot passage, and they were completely exhausted.

The night went by fast; Rita was the first one up. She walked outside the cave and jumped into the water to refresh herself.

She went swimming out as far as she could to see if she may perhaps locate the cave where the treasure was alleged to be. She looked around but there was no sign of any caves. She swam back to the cave and woke Jason up.

She had related to him that she did not see any cave entrance above the cave that they were in. "You can't see it. It's above us," Jason replied, while he stretched out. Jason woke Cyrus up and told him that they had to get started and to fully inflate the two dinghies.

"Let get some breakfast first," Samantha suggested.

"We don't have time for breakfast. We can't waste any time," Cyrus told her.

He couldn't wait to get his hands on the Maltese Falcon. Jason was trying to inflate the dinghy, but he couldn't figure how to do it. Cyrus neared Jason and pulled back the cap and the dinghy inflated up. "I've never seen anything like that before." An astonished Jason bounced back. Cyrus dragged the dinghy into the water while Jason carried some of the supplies to load them on.

Cyrus asked Jason, "Do we need all of this stuff to take with us?"

"No, all we need is the flashlights, the harpoon, and the rope ladder, the batteries and the folded dinghy. Don't forget to bring the bottled water also," Jason said as he double-checked on the supplies. The scent of gasoline got Jason's attention.

He looked inside the dinghy and noted that the bottom of the dinghy was completely wet with gasoline; he touched the rope ladder and noticed that it was soaked with gasoline. "Why is the rope ladder soaked with gasoline?" Jason asked Cyrus.

Cyrus explained to Jason that one of the gasoline tanks had been leaking. Jason, somewhat doubtful, looked inside the dinghy and found that definitely the portable plastic gas tank was leaking. Jason was speculative as to how the gas tank was punctured in the first place. Jason wasn't sure whether to believe Cyrus or not and told Cyrus to keep the rope ladder and the rest of the ropes away from any fire.

Cyrus took a deep breath and looked at Samantha and said to her, "Wow, that was close one, thanks for your help."

"You didn't tell me anything of your planning, how am I supposed to know what you are up to? So don't blame me. You told me not to ask any questions," whispered Samantha as she walked away from Cyrus.

Cyrus grabbed Samantha by her arms and said, "Don't be anxious, after today, it will all be over for him, and it will be a new beginning for us."

Jason and Rita were in the dinghy waiting for them. "Come on, you two," shouted Jason. "We have to go." Cyrus and Samantha ran and got into the dinghy.

They rowed to the middle of the bay, and Jason instructed everyone to look for a cave entrance up high, as he was rowing the dinghy. Not long after Jason noticed a huge hole in the cliff up and said, "There it is, up there." He pointed to everyone's attention.

The other three looked up. "Where is it? I don't see anything," restlessly asked Cyrus.

"How many big holes do you see up there?" Jason questioned.

"Well, I can only see one that looks like a cave entrance. However, if that is the one, it is too far up for us to climb up," Cyrus replied.

"Well, I have pleasant news and bad news. The pleasant news is that's the one, and the bad news is that we have to get up there then look for the Falcon," Jason replied.

Samantha got very fearful, and she told them that she had no intention to climb up that high to the entrance, "Oh, my God, I am not going up there," Samantha said nervously. Jason told her that if she makes a decision to stay behind that she has to go back to the cave and had to wait for them until they return.

"She will come up," said Cyrus, as he gave an angry look to Samantha. They rowed back to the main cave to get the other dinghy that was loaded with the supplies that they would need to start the search for the Maltese Falcon. Jason told Cyrus to bring with them the hand shovels, in case they had to do any deep digging. Cyrus recommended that it would be better to tie the two rope ladders with each other because the entrance was too high up for the length of one. Jason agreed; he cut up some pieces of rope to tie the ladders with each other. They joined the dinghy that was loaded with supplies to the back of theirs and rowed back out to the middle of the bay. Once they got into the area, Jason attached one end of the rope ladder to the harpoon and tied a large hook to the rope ladder. Jason aimed towards the cave entrance and shot up the harpoon. The hook shot up dragging the ladder, but it didn't come close to the cave. The hook and the rope ladder tumbled down into the water.

"Damn," Jason said. "We have to get closer."

He tried about four times, but he wasn't successful at getting to his objective. Jason asked Cyrus to row closer underneath the cave; he aimed one more time and blasted the harpoon. This was their fifth try and their lucky five; the hook got hooked over the edge of the cave. Jason pulled down on the rope to see if it was strongly secured to take their weight. "Alright," said Jason with a smile. "It appears secure enough. I will go up first, and I will take the rope with me. Tie the supplies to it and I will haul the supplies up," said Jason, and he started to climb up, then he stopped and told them that once he reached the top, and entered inside the cave, the girls will come up one at a time. He looked at Cyrus and said to him, "Cyrus, before you climb up, tie the dinghy to the ladder so it will not drift away, and tie the other one to the rope."

"Why? Don't tell me you are bringing the dinghy up there? What for? There can't be any water up there," Cyrus kept asking Jason.

"We don't know what's up there. We might need it. I don't want to just tie it up," quickly replied Jason while he started to slowly climb the ladder. It was very difficult for Jason to climb the ladder because it was soaked with the gasoline. It made his grip slippery, and the fumes of the gasoline were making his eyes burn. It took great effort for Jason to reach the top; finally, he stepped inside the cave.

He looked around the cave. "What a place to hide a treasure," he said to himself. He looked below and threw the end of the rope down to Cyrus. Cyrus tied one of the dinghies to the rope and gave the signal to Jason to pull it up. Once Jason had pulled the dinghy up into the cave, Rita started to climb up. Samantha kept firmly telling Cyrus that she didn't want to climb up.

"Now you listen to me; you have to go up with me. I will need your backing. That is, if you want to share the fortune from the Falcon. So don't be scared. In a few minutes, we are going to be rich," Cyrus encouraged Samantha. Cyrus gave Samantha a gentle lift to reach the ladder. He knew that once he mentioned money to her that she would do anything, no matter what. Samantha had built sufficient bravery and started climbing up the rope ladder slowly. Jason and Rita sat down on the ground waiting for Samantha. "Well, this is very interesting. I wonder how he used to come up here," she asked.

"That is a good question," Jason replied. "And I wonder how he used to bring the women slaves up here also. That's why I think that there is another entrance somewhere else, and it's not on the maps." Samantha made it to the top, and she begged for help.

Jason and Rita reached out for her and helped her to get inside. Cyrus climbed up after her. Once they all rested, Jason suggested to get started. "Let's leave the dinghy here, just bring the shovels and the flashlights along," Jason said as he led the way.

The cave entrance was extremely wide, the back of the cave funnels, and it was separate from two different directions. Each one of them picked up a flashlight and started to walk towards to the back of the cave. Jason leading turned towards the left as it showed on the map. It got very dark; unexpectedly, the girls started to scream aloud.

"What happened?" Jason asked looking in the rear at the girls as they were holding each other. Jason walked towards Samantha and Rita and noted four human skeletons chained to the wall. "They won't bother us, let's keep on going," he told them. They followed Jason deeper into the cave. It wasn't long after the small pathway that they were following finished into another smaller cave. Jason pointed the flashlight on the map and told the others that according to the map that was the location where the Falcon should be hidden. There were small holes within the cave, and the Falcon could be in one of the holes. With the flashlight in their hands, they looked inside the hollow holes and all they found were skeletons' bones.

"Damn, all of this for nothing," Cyrus said, getting very irritated.

"We might be a hundred years too late, perhaps someone else got to it before us," Jason said in disappointment.

Samantha sat down angry, and she started pointing the flashlight around the cave walls. Suddenly, she shone the light on a hole at the bottom corner of the cave, "Look, there is something shining in there," she yelled. "There is something in that hole," she kept repeating.

Jason and Cyrus crouched down. Jason reached inside the hole and started to fondle inside. He extended his arm inside, and he felt something with the tip of his fingers.

Quickly, Rita handed to Jason her flashlight and Jason shone the light inside the hole. There it was: a two-foot statue of a golden bird entirely covered with dust and cobwebs. "I'll be damned! It is true; it does exist," Jason yelled with intense excitement.

Cyrus crawled to his knees to look inside the hole, and he could not believe his eyes. "We found it. We found it!" screamed Cyrus while he jumped up and down.

"Let me see it," Rita asked eagerly. She pointed the light on the golden bird. "Oh, my God," she said. "That is absolutely beautiful!"

Jason tried to get a grasp the golden statue to pull it out. The statue was out of reach. As a result, he could not get a firm hold of it. The hole was slightly too small for Jason and Cyrus to try to squeeze in; it was also relatively tiny for Rita and Samantha. The statue was there is the front of them, but out of their real accomplishment. All they could do was just sit and look at it. Sweaty and frustrated, Cyrus started yelling at Jason to do something given that he was in command. "What are we going to do? None of us can reach it, and we don't have any tools to make the hole bigger." Cyrus leaned against the cave's wall.

Rita told Cyrus to calm down. "We need to rest and be calm. With yelling and rage, we will never get out of the situation that we're in."

Jason was sitting down on the ground resting with his back against the cool wall of the cave. Gently, he told them that he had an idea of how to get the bird out of the cage.

The rest of them asked. "What type of suggestion do you have?" eagerly Rita asked.

"Cyrus, you have to go back to the cave and bring one sleeping bag and the two oars," Jason ordered Cyrus.

"For what? Don't tell me you are planning to sleep up here until that statue walks out by itself," Cyrus replied. At this moment, he was very angry and discouraged. He was furious because Jason was ordering him around just like Richard did, and discouraged because standing around, he would never accomplish his plan.

"Do you want the Maltese Falcon? If so, do as I say," Jason told Cyrus with a treating manner. The four of them returned to the entrance of the cave. Cyrus climbed down the ladder and got into the dinghy and rowed back to the cave where they had started. He loaded the sleeping bags into the dinghy and returned into the cave. Cyrus wrapped the sleeping bags around the oars and tied them together to the end to the rope that was hanging from the top of the cave. He pulled the rope to signal to Jason to pull up. Cyrus reached the top before Jason could pull up the sleeping bags.

"Let me give you a hand," Cyrus told Jason, and he helped Jason to pull up the load.

"That was swift! You sure go up rapidly enough," Jason complimented Cyrus.

"Yes, I know. It is getting dark, and I wanted to make sure that I got over here before it darkens. I am surreally excited, and I want to make sure that everything goes well for Richard."

Jason looked at Cyrus in astonishment, and suddenly he started to get bad thoughts about Cyrus's performance; he sensed that something was going on in Cyrus's brains. The four of them returned to the area where the statue was. Jason knelt down and asked for a flashlight. He opened the sleeping bag and shoved in with the oar and spread it around the statue. Rita asked Jason what he was trying to do.

"Since none of us can reach the statue, then we have to bring the statue to us," replied Jason as he stood up.

"Now what?" Samantha asked. "Are you going to put the statue to sleep?" Samantha laughed.

"Shut up. Just shut up," yelled Cyrus at Samantha. "He brought us this far, and he knows exactly what he is doing."

Samantha got bewildered with Cyrus's action, and she was wondering what he was planning to do once, or if, they got to the statue.

Once the sleeping bags were around the statue, Jason threw out a rope around the statue neck, slowly he pulled back and the bird fell down on the sleeping bag. Jason tried to pull the sleeping bag by himself, but it was too heavy.

"Give me a hand, Cyrus, this sucker is too heavy," said Jason. Cyrus pushed Samantha out of his way so he could help Jason. Cyrus and Jason pulled extremely hard trying to get the statue out of the hole. It was not a worry-free task because the ground was rugged. The sleeping bag kept getting wedged on the edges of the sharp, rough rocks.

When they eventually pulled the Falcon out of the hole, Jason laid back on the ground. At the same time, Cyrus and Samantha began to stroke the golden statue.

Rita looked at them and asked if they were planning to have sex with the Falcon. She knelt down and commenced to dust off some of the dirt of the statue. She could see the beaming of the gold with every clean.

Rita asked Jason if the Maltese Falcon statue was solid gold. Jason smiled and told her that she was dusting up the most prestigious solid gold statue in the world. Cyrus didn't take his eyes off the statue while at the same time he was planning his revenge.

"Sure is, that is why it is valued so great a deal of money," replied Jason. "We don't have time to admire the statue. You will have lots of time to see it a lot better once we properly clean it up. Let's get everything together and let's get out of here."

Jason cautioned them not to leave anything behind them. "Now the problem is, we have to carry it out," said Jason. He asked Rita to hand him the two oars.

"What are you going to do with the oars?" asked Cyrus.

Jason told Cyrus that they had to make a stretcher. Jason cut a hole at the end of each corner of the sleeping bag and shoved an oar on each side. Slowly, they laid the statue down on the stretcher; Jason and Cyrus lifted up the stretcher with the golden bird on it.

"Samantha, go in front of Cyrus to lead the way; and, Rita, come behind me and keeps those flashlights pointed at the ground, so we won't fall," Jason directly ordered.

"This must weight over two hundred pounds," commented Cyrus.

They walked very slowly. It was complicated getting out of the cave, especially when the ground was wet from the dripping water that was coming down from the cave ceiling. Jason and Cyrus had to be extra careful where to put their steps, since they were doing the carrying, they were not able to carry a flashlight, and it was not easy to see where they were going.

Chapter19
The Double-Cross

Finally, they arrived at the cave entrance. "We'll take a short rest and, afterwards, we have got to find a way to bring this down to the dinghy," said Jason as he sat down.

The bright sun was still shining on the cave entrance; Rita took a closer look at the golden bird. "Look at all these diamonds!" Rita exclaimed.

"Yeah, look at them," said Cyrus as he pulled a gun and held it to Rita's head.

"What the hell is going on?" questioned Jason while he stepped towards Cyrus.

"Don't take another step, or I'll waste her," screamed Cyrus. "Move your back against the wall and put your hands up where I can see them, bum boy."

"I knew it. I had truly terrible feelings about you. I should not at any time have trusted you," said Jason while he raised his hands up and inclined against the cave's wall. Cyrus ordered Samantha to tie Jason's hands behind his back. Samantha cautiously walked towards Jason and asked him to turn around and face the wall. Samantha slowly went behind Jason, and told him to put his hands behind his back. He did as she asked. Cyrus instructed Samantha to make sure that she tied Jason's hands very tight as he smiled.

Rita tried to get away from Cyrus, but he managed to put his arms around her throat and nearly choked her.

"He is all done, now, what about the cookie?" Samantha asked Cyrus as she pointed at Rita.

"I have plans for the rich spoiled bitch," Cyrus replied. Rita managed to luckily escape Cyrus's choke hold, and quickly she ran towards Samantha. Samantha saw her approaching and as soon as Rita got near to her, Samantha jabbed Rita on her jaw. Rita fell down to the ground totally unconscious.

"Wow, what a right punch," laughed Cyrus.

When Jason saw Rita on the floor, he ran towards her. You could see the anger upon his face. He knelt down and started to call Rita's name. His hands tied behind his back, he could not do anything to help out Rita. Cyrus gingerly approached Jason, grabbed him from his throat, and pulled him up to his feet. As soon as Jason was on his feet, he kicked Cyrus's gun away from his hand. He tried to wrestle Cyrus and wildly kept kicking him. Cyrus got himself cornered as Jason kept kicking Cyrus's legs.

Cyrus called Samantha to help him. She picked up a rock, crept behind Jason and struck him on the back of his head with the rock. Jason fell down to the ground as blood started gushing out from his head.

"Let's get the hell out of this place and bring that sleeping bag over nearby," Cyrus told Samantha. Cyrus wrapped the statue with the sleeping bag and tied the sleeping bag to the end of the rope.

"You go down in the dinghy, and I will lower the statue slowly. Make sure to bring the dinghy underneath it." Samantha climbed down the ladder, got into the dinghy and waited for Cyrus to lower down the statue. Cyrus could not lift the golden bird by himself, so he dragged it up to the edge of the cave. He attempted to lower the statue down, but it was too heavy to handle it by himself. As soon as he placed the statue on the edge of the cave the statue tumbled down off the edge into the water. Samantha was waiting in the dinghy, but when she saw the statue falling down fast, she jumped out from the dinghy. The statue hit the water and made a big splash. The only thing that stopped the statue from sinking toward the bottom of the sea was the end to the rope got knotted around a rock at the cave's edge. Cyrus was stunned; he ran down the rope ladder. Half-way down he jumped from the ladder into the water to try to stop the statue from sinking. He swam towards Samantha as she was holding to the dinghy.

"I thought you said that you were going to lower it slowly? What are you trying to do, kill me?" asked Samantha while trying to get back into the dinghy.

"It's too heavy; I couldn't hold it," Cyrus replied. He pulled the dinghy nearer to where the statue was dangling. He could see the glitter of the gold on the water surface; he tried to lift it up, but it was too heavy for him to handle.

"We have to pull it up before the rope unravels and it sinks," said Cyrus.

"How are you going to do that? You couldn't even hold it, let alone lift it up," angrily Samantha replied.

"Don't worry, I will go up again, and I will try to pull it up. Once it clears the water surface you push the dinghy underneath the statue," said Cyrus, and he started to climb up to the cave.

When he arrived closer to the top, he was worried that Jason could have recovered from the hit to the head. Cautiously, he looked around the cave; Rita and Jason were still both unconscious and lying upon the ground. Cyrus pulled the rope; he only managed to raise the statue up to a couple of inches. Samantha tried hard to push the dinghy underneath the statue and tried to lift it up, but all her effort was all in vain. "Pull up some more," she yelled as she was getting frustrated.

Cyrus tried his hardest, but the statue was too heavy for him to pull it out of the water. Samantha yelled and told Cyrus to stop pulling up because she had an idea. Cyrus wasn't in a position to quarrel or inquire about Samantha's idea. He was getting tired holding onto the rope, and he yelled down to Samantha to hurry up and to do something fast.

"Pull up as much as you can," she yelled again. Cyrus captured a deep breath, grabbed the rope, raised his legs against the wall, and started to pull. He gave all the power that he had left in him; he managed to pull it up enough that the bottom of the statue was above the water. Samantha yelled at him to hold it where it was, she jumped out of the dinghy, she pushed the edge of the dinghy down and pushed it underneath the hanging statue. "It worked," said Samantha to herself. She shouted and told Cyrus that it worked and told Cyrus to lower the statue very slowly. With the golden bird resting in the dinghy, Cyrus ran to the edge and looked below.

"I'll be damned; it worked," mumbled Cyrus to himself. He looked back and saw that Rita started to move. He threw down the rope and made his way down the rope ladder to the dinghy. Once Cyrus reached the bottom, he got into the dinghy.

"We did it!" Samantha said as she passionately kissed Cyrus.

"Stop, we have to get out of here fast," said Cyrus. They pulled the dinghy with the statue on it closer to theirs, and Cyrus helped Samantha to get inside it. They secured both dinghies together and rowed a few feet away from where the rope ladder was still hanging from the top of the cave.

Cyrus reached inside one of the dinghy pockets and pulled out a box of matches wrapped in a plastic a bag. "Wait here!" he told Samantha, as he swam towards the rope ladder; he floated on his back keeping the matches above the water not to get wet.

As soon he arrived at the rope ladder, Cyrus ignited a match and placed it against the rope ladder. Before long, the burning match touched the ladder and it caught on fire so rapid that Cyrus nearly burnt his hand from the flames. The fires dispersed to the top of the rope; the burning remnants of the ladder fell into the water. Cyrus looked upward towards the cave entrance as he swam back to the dinghy. There was not any indication that any of the ladder was still untouched by the fire and there was not enough at all left for Jason and Rita to get down from the cave.

"This is why you poured gasoline on it?" Samantha said as she smiled. Cyrus did not say a word and kept rowing the dinghy back to the main cave.

As they reached the cave entrance, Samantha got out from the dinghy; she started to remove her clothes and got naked. She ran towards Cyrus and pressed him down to the ground, and she got on top of Cyrus and started to unfasten his pants. Cyrus shoved Samantha off him and told her to put her clothes on: he continued to tell her that he was in no state of mind for sex at that moment. Samantha got really angry and walked back where she dropped her clothes and got dressed. She asked Cyrus how the two of them may carry the statue back to the yacht. Cyrus told her that he would use Jason's idea by making a stretcher with the oars and the sleeping bag that he left behind at the cave.

As Cyrus was putting together the stretcher, Samantha asked, "Do you honestly think that they will make it out from that cave?"

"You look as if you are worried, or you care about them," replied Cyrus.

"No, I don't care about them, let's presume they make it down, and they inform Richard everything? By the way, how are going to explain to Richard their sudden disappearance?" Samantha asked timidly.

"How do you assume that they will come down from that cave? In addition, I have a surprise for Richard as well. I told you, babe, this one was for us only and nobody will share with us," Cyrus replied as he kissed Samantha.

When Cyrus finished assembling the stretcher, he laid down the Falcon on it as they got prepared to go through the passage opening. It was very complicated for Samantha and Cyrus carrying the heavy statue. They had to tie the flashlights around their waists to see their way into the dark passage.

They had to be incredibly careful where to step for they had a minimum amount of light from the flashlights, and they could barely see the walking trail. Cyrus and Samantha made relatively frequent stops because Samantha was becoming tired, and both were getting thirsty. The high temperature inside the passage made both slow moving.

With all the excitement, they forgot to carry with them some bottled water, as they never thought about anything else. All they cared about was the golden statue and to get out of that cave. As well, they left all the supplies behind them back in the cave. Finally, they made it to where they had started at the beginning with the search.

As soon as they reached the end of the passage and entered into the larger cave, both dropped down to the ground, as they were quite exhausted.

They had no time to refresh themselves by a swim as they heard voices heading in their direction.

"Get in here so nobody will see us," said Cyrus while pulling Samantha from her arms to hide behind a large rock, as a tour boat was entering the cave.

Cyrus waited for the tour boat to exit the area, and he whispered to Samantha, "This is what we have to do. We will leave the bird here."

Samantha did not let Cyrus to continue. "What if somebody sees it?"

Cyrus assured her that no one would ever see the treasure. "Now you listen to me just like I told you before, do as I say and don't ask any questions. We will swim to the yacht. Better yet, I'll swim to the yacht, and you'll wait here. I will shortly return to pick up you and the Falcon." Cyrus sneaked from behind the rock and looked around, and he made sure that the tour boat was gone.

Chapter 20
The Murder

He jumped into the water and started swimming towards the yacht where Richard was patiently waiting.

Half way to the yacht Cyrus started to yell "Richard, Richard!" Cyrus kept screaming as he was swimming towards the yacht. Richard heard the yelling, looked around, and saw Cyrus swimming quickly towards the yacht. Richard assisted Cyrus to get on board the yacht and without any hesitation asked, "Where are the others? What happened? Where are the others?" Richard kept asking.

Cyrus started to moan softly and kept telling Richard repeatedly that he couldn't do anything. "I tried; I couldn't get them out. It was just terrible." Cyrus made Richard believe that he was in tremendous shock.

Richard became alarmed, and rushed to the bar and brought a bottle of rum and poured a glass and handed it to Cyrus. He carried on telling Cyrus to relax and gave him another glass of rum. "Now, tell me what the hell happened out there? Where are the others?" Richard asked Cyrus.

Cyrus calmly started saying, "Halfway into the cave, rocks started falling down, we ran into different directions, Jason was leading, and Rita was behind him. I heard the rumbling, and then I saw everybody running I ran to the entrance. When the rumbling stopped I went back in the cave but the entrance was blocked with this a huge rock. I couldn't do anything, and I had to come back." Cyrus's fabrication made Richard believe in his story.

"What happened to the others?" asked Richard. "What about Rita?" Richard asked again.

"Richard, they are all dead. Let's get out of here," Cyrus suggested.

"Cyrus, we have to go back and look for them. We cannot just leave them in there. Maybe they are still alive. My daughter is in there!" Richard said while he kept staring towards the cave entrance.

"Boss, it is impossible for anyone to survive. Those huge rocks probably had crushed all of them. If you demand to go in there trying looking for them, we have to go and get some help. You and I alone will not be able to do anything," said Cyrus anticipating to convince Richard not to return into to cave.

Richard told Cyrus that they had go to the mainland and get help to search for the rest of them. Richard was all shaken up and under lots of great pressure, and did not very well know what to do. At that difficult moment, he had forgotten about the Maltese Falcon; his main concern was his daughter Rita. Richard started the engine, pulled the anchor up and steered away from the cave, all confused not knowing which direction to go. Richard shut off the engine and called Cyrus over to talk to him. Cyrus pretended that he was too exhausted and stayed sitting at the table. Richard was all disarranged and had no clue where they had to go for help. His main trouble was in what manner he was going to explain the situation to the authorities.

Cyrus felt comfortable knowing that Richard believed him while Richard was passing back and forth, trying to think of an excuse to tell the authorities. Cyrus was getting annoyed with Richard's delay; he called Richard over. "Come look at this," Cyrus yelled as he was leaning over the side of the yacht.

Richard walked towards Cyrus and asked, "What are you looking at?" Cyrus was still leaning over the railing asked Richard to hurry up. Richard ran towards Cyrus and asked what all the fuss was about.

"Down here look. You have to see this, quick," said Cyrus.

Richard leant over the railing and asked, "What? What are you looking at? I don't see anything."

Cyrus pulled a knife and stabbed Richard in the back of his neck; Richard fell down in a puddle of blood. Cyrus knelt beside Richard's bloody body, doomed Richard for all the mistreatment Cyrus received from him and stabbed Richard repeatedly until Cyrus got tired. Cyrus, covered with Richard's blood, picked up Richard's dead body and tossed him overboard. In a matter of seconds, Richard's body disappeared into the water. Cyrus washed the blood off the deck, and then he dived in into water to wash the blood off himself. He started the engine and turned the yacht back to the cave where he left Samantha waiting. Once he arrived at the cave entrance, Cyrus lowered the small boat and steered it towards the cave.

Samantha waited patiently for Cyrus to come back for her. She had no idea of what kind of surprise Cyrus had for Richard. She watched the yacht anchoring far away from outside the cave as she saw Cyrus going her way with the small motor boat. Once Cyrus got near her, she did not waste any time. "What the hell took you so long?" she yelled at Cyrus.

"Never mind the yelling. You will find out soon. Let's get out of here fast," Cyrus replied. They lowered the statue into the boat, and they went back to the yacht.

"Where is Richard?" Samantha asked eagerly.

"Oh, he had an accident. At the time, I got to the yacht; he was drunk; he didn't even clearly recognize me. I went down below to get some supplies and when I came up on deck he was gone," Cyrus told Samantha.

"You are lying. I know you are. Tell me, what did you do to Richard?" Samantha asked.

Cyrus didn't know if Samantha was really serious as she looked; he got prepared for the worst scenario, therefore, he told her the truth. For a moment Samantha seemed stunned for a while, but it didn't take her long to celebrate. "You mean it is just you and me? The two of us, all alone, and no Richard?" Samantha started laughing and jumping up and down with joy. Both were ecstatically happy because they were all just them, the Maltese Falcon, the yacht, and Richard's money.

Cyrus looked at Samantha and told her, "Remember, I promised you that this treasure is ours. I also keep my promises."

Cyrus managed to drag the statue below to his cabin, and Samantha followed. "We have to get away from this island," Cyrus said as he lay on his bed.

Samantha lay beside him and asked, "Why don't we leave now and head back to the States?" She started to stroke Cyrus's penis.

"We can't do that. The harbour officials will want to know where the others are; besides we cannot leave the crew behind. We have to hide for a while. I have a few contacts I need to make connection with to help us find a purchaser for this golden bird, furthermore, I do not know by what means to sail this thing back to the States. I am not a sea captain." Cyrus at no time made any plans of what to do once he had power over the Falcon. He required some time to clear his head from all the hostility now that he got what he wanted.

"We will go to the marina and discharge the crew. We'll give them a fair amount of money to buy a plane ticket to the States, pay off their salary, and then we can sell the yacht," proposed Cyrus.

"Well, I hope you are aware of what you are doing. Do not forget, we have the Maltese Falcon. What are we going to do with it?" Samantha asked curiously.

"Do you have to enquire so many questions at one time? I can't think when you do that," replied Cyrus, all frustrated knowing that Samantha was accurate and that he hadn't at all made a well thought-out plan.

"Let's return to the marina and afterwards, we have to think of something." Cyrus sailed to the marina without having any indication what to do next.

Chapter 21
The Escape

Back in the cave, Rita was trying to stand up, but she was shaky.

She attempted various times to stand; she was incapable of doing so. She managed to front crawl and pushed herself to lean next to the cave's wall.

Rita didn't have a clue where she was, looked around the cave to establish her location. Her vision was out of focus and the sunlight shining through the cave entrance disturbed her vision. She rested for a moment. Rita opened her eyes and tried to get to her senses. Slowly, she turned her head from side to side; that's when she realized where she was. She called Jason's name a few times. She glanced around the cave when Rita saw Jason's body lying face-down, and his head covered with blood. She crawled towards him and grabbed Jason from his shoulder, "Jason, Jason," she yelled while she was shaking him.

Rita could not comprehend what occurred; woozy, she slowly turned around and lay with her back beside Jason. After a period of time, she started to come to her senses and managed to get up on her feet. Slowly, she walked toward the stream of water that was flowing from the cave's ceiling; she bowed her head and let the water dribble on her face. The cold, clear water re-energized Rita. After a while, she believed that she could control herself to walk. She strolled close to Jason, released Jason's hands, and turned him face up. "What a bump!" Rita said to herself at the same time touched

Jason's head. She took her t-shirt off and soaked it under the stream. She let her shirt get soaked so she could wrap Jason's head.

Rita wrapped Jason's head with her wet shirt and, at the same time, she wiped the dried blood from her chin. After a while, Jason started to move, he opened his eyes and said slowly, "Where am I? What happened to me?"

"We are up in the cave and have you been smacked with a rock on the back of your head. The other two took off," Rita replied.

"Took off?" Jason asked as he tried little by little to get up to his feet with Rita's help. Once Jason was on his feet and could control his balance, Rita helped him towards the stream. Jason put his head underneath the water, and he stood underneath the dripping water to re-establish his senses. In the meantime, Rita walked close to the cave's edge, and as soon as she arrived, she looked down.

With a dismayed gaze upon her face, she put her head between her hands, and sobbed. "Oh no; we are condemned. We are going to die up here." Rita could not believe what she had observed.

"What are you talking about?" Jason asked, as he walked towards the cave's edge where Rita was standing in bewilderment. He looked down. "Oh my god. That son of a bitch burnt the rope ladder. How in the hell we are going to get out of this place?" he asked as his eyes filled with tears.

Rita started to cry and she told Jason, "We are going to die up here. No one will at any time find us, and nobody knows where we are."

Jason rested over the cave's edge and snapped a piece of what was left of the rope ladder. He examined it and noticed that the ladder had been burnt out. Crushing the small piece of burnt rope around his hand, he yelled, "I'll kill them. I vow to god that I am going to kill those three." He turned towards Rita and told her, "And if I discover that you have something to do with this, I'll kill you too."

Jason was distressed. He put his hands around Rita's throat, started squeezing her throat so hard that Rita could hardly gasp for air.

"Jason, let me go. Let go. You are hurting me, and I can't breathe," she yelled at Jason, and she was punching and kicking Jason; she was fighting for her life. Jason soon realized what he was doing, let go of Rita's and walked away from her.

Rita tried to gasp for air to scream at Jason. "How can I be implicated? If I conspired with them, then what the hell I am doing up here abandoned with you, lunatic bustard?" She dropped down to her knees and began to weep.

Jason stood silent, did not know what to say nor how to express regret for his actions. He looked at Rita with tears in his eyes, and slowly he turned towards her, knelt down to his knees, and said, "I am very sorry; you are right. I lost my head. Knowing exaltedly that we won't to be able to get out of this cave got me hallucinating." Jason helped Rita to stand up, and they walked towards the edge of the cave, and they looked down at the sea surface. Knowing that there was no other way out, they realized that the cave might end up being there grave site.

"Maybe somebody will come upon us," said Rita, staring at the sea down below.

"Find us, up here? Look around you, Rita, and tell me what you see?" asked Jason in a tender, mumbling voice.

"Do you see these skeletons? Do you know how long they have been up here? Does it look like anyone has found them?" Jason stood silent. The thought of Cyrus came to mind; Jason came to realize that Cyrus meant what he said to him when Cyrus made the comment, "If I don't kill you first." The thought about Cyrus energized Jason's mental state of mind. One thing he yearned for: revenge.

Jason started to pace back and forth. Dying up in that cave was the only conclusion if they didn't find a way out. He sat down. He broke the silence and whimpered, "We have no food, no water and no way out. We are going to die up here."

"Please, don't talk like that!" Rita begged with tears in her eyes. She ran towards Jason. Jason hugged Rita; with his arms around her, she felt some comfort.

Jason asked her to stop crying and to concentrate on finding a way out from that condemned cave as he aided Rita to sit down. Jason wiped the tears from Rita's face. He stood up and walked towards the leftover supplies that Cyrus left behind. He looked at the folded dinghy and said with half a smile, "What goes up must go down." He pulled the cap and inflated the dinghy.

"What are you talking about?" Rita asked at the same time she walked towards him.

"Look at this. There is enough rope, and we have this dinghy. All we have to do is use this dinghy as a glider," Jason said as Rita looked at Jason in a strange look.

"What do mean as a glider? How can we use a dinghy as a glider? It's only a dinghy; dinghies float on water, they don't fly in the air," Rita explained with humour.

Jason smiled. "I am glad that you found your sense of humour, but if we turn this dinghy upside down and put restraint ropes around it, we would be able to jump from here and the dinghy will serve as a parachute," Jason replied.

"You mean we will have to jump? From up here, with a dinghy over our head? Oh no, it is too high. That would be a suicide. It will not work, and I am not going to jump. If you want to jump with a dinghy over your head, you go first. Once you make a splash, afterwards you go get some help," Rita replied all shaken up and scared. She was hoping that Jason was only teasing her about his idea of jumping.

"What if I don't survive the jump? In that situation, what are you going to do? You're forced to stay up here by yourself, just you and the skeletons, then what?" Jason asked Rita. He continued. "Let's say I survive the jump, where do you want me to go to get help and how am I supposed to explain why we are up here? I'd rather die trying to get out from this cave than I spend the rest of my life in a Maltese jail. Listen to me, we can't stay up here," insisted Jason as he started tying the ropes around it.

"I presently can't believe my dad would do such a thing to me," Rita said as she started to help Jason tying the ropes around the dinghy.

"Perhaps he has nothing to do with this scam. Maybe Cyrus made up a story and told Richard that we died, or we had some kind of accident. Alternatively, he is after your dad as well. This way, he can keep the treasure for himself and Samantha. Right now, I am not concerned about them; I just want to get out of here so I can kill all three of them," as he pulled on the rope to tie it.

"My first expedition with my Dad, and we're getting to be acquainted with each after all the absence between us," Rita calmly said.

"Once I catch up with them, this would be the last trip that your dad will ever have, if this was his plan," Jason said, tying knots in the rope.

"You wouldn't hurt him, would you?" Rita asked worriedly. "You just finished telling me that you didn't think that my dad had anything to do with this." Rita was not pleased with the comments that Jason made about killing all three of them; that included her dad.

"Harm him? Now, let us see; we are left abandoned up in this cave when they very well knew that there is no other way out of this cave, and to leave us up here to have a slow death. No I won't hurt him; I'll kill him. Only, of course, if he had something to do with this inconvenience." Jason stopped because he could sense the anger starting to build up inside him. He remained silently looking at Rita, observing a beautiful, innocent, child-like woman abounded by her father and left to die in a cave for the sake of money, yet she still believed that he was innocent. What kind of a father would do something horrifying to his only daughter, and how could a parent like that live the rest of his life without a troubled conscience? You could see the anger in Jason's face as he finished tying the last rope around the dinghy.

"Okay, all we have to do is to get up on the edge and grasp on to these ropes and jump," Jason said, while carrying the dinghy over his head towards the edge of the cave.

Rita immobilized. "Are you certain it will work?" she asked.

"No, I'm not sure. There is only one way to determine if it works," answered Jason. "One way or another, we are going to die, so might as well die trying to get out from this cave alive and hope for the best." Jason walked on the cave's edge, holding the dinghy over his head. "Are you coming or are you going to join these skeletons, because I am not," Jason yelled at Rita.

Rita slowly climbed up beside Jason; shaken and trembling, she put her arms around him. She looked at Jason and told him that she was very frightened.

"That makes two of us," Jason replied, calmly realizing that this could be the end of their lives. Trying to deliver Rita some encouragement, he told her that they needed a bath. "Come on, just take a deep breath, and jump," he instructed Rita.

"No, no, I can't!" Rita cried out. "I am scared."

Jason was getting impatient as he attempted to explain to Rita that if they don't do anything that they would have a slow and harrowing death of starvation or take the jump, hit the water and die instantly. "Rita, look at me, you have to hold on to these ropes and don't let go until we are in the water.

It is going to work, and we will have a safe landing." Jason held Rita's hand and led them to the ropes.

"That's right, hold tight. I tell you something, I am truly terrified too but don't you want to get even with Samantha after all she knocked you out cold with one punch?" Jason said, trying to give Rita a motivation to jump. Rita got some courage and did what Jason asked her to do. She took a hold of the rope, and with both hands, she squeezed the ropes tight.

Jason took a deep breath and grabbed on the ropes. "Whatever you do, don't let go of the ropes. On the count of three," Jason said. As he looked at the blameless face of Rita, he couldn't resist the temptation; he turned his face towards Rita and kissed her. They looked at each other, took a deep breath and Jason started the count. "One, two, three." On the count of three they jumped. Rita screamed and Jason screeched as they were gliding very slowly just as Jason thought they would. Half-way down, the rope ripped off one side of the dinghy and split the dinghy in half, both fell down into the water. Once Jason hit the water, he started laughing. "We made it. Wasn't that fun?" yelled Jason, knowing that he survived the fall, and he looked around for Rita. He did not see her. Fearfully, Jason yelled her name as loud. It traumatized Jason; he kept yelling Rita's name. Suddenly, he heard her voice, "I am over here, get me out of here!"

Jason happily yelled, "Where are you?"

"Here, under this stupid dinghy," Rita answered.

Jason saw the other half of the dinghy, and he swam towards it; he lifted it off Rita's head. She was still holding on to the ropes. Rita smiled at Jason. "You are crazy one son of a bitch."

"You haven't seen madness yet. You can let go of the ropes now; I hope that you know how to swim," Jason told her as he helped Rita to let loose from the rope that she was holding.

They swam back to the main cave. Once they reached the entrance, they noticed that Cyrus left behind most of the supplies, excluding the flashlights.

"I guess we have to find our way out in the dark," Rita expressed to Jason.

"Yes, we are going to; we have no alternative." Jason and Rita made their way into the darkness of the passage. Both knew that it was going to be a rugged way out, especially without any light to see their way. Fortunately, for them, Cyrus left the water bottles behind.

Jason told Rita to grab a couple of water bottles because they were going to need them once they made their way into the interior of the passage.

Chapter 22
Hide Away

Cyrus and Samantha entered the marina and anchored the yacht. "The first thing we have to do is to look for some cash," Cyrus informed Samantha. They knew that Richard carried large sums of cash with him when he travelled. They proceeded down to Richard's cabin, and Samantha knew exactly where Richard put aside the money. She opened the desk drawer and took the key for the safe. Once she opened the safe, she could not believe her eyes. She called Cyrus over. "Look at all this money!" Cyrus exclaims.

"There must be over a million dollars in there," Samantha said.

"Half a million was presumed to go to Jason," said Cyrus, cheerful.

"Now all we have to do is to get rid of the captain and the crew," said Cyrus.

"No, no, more killing," Samantha sorrowfully told Cyrus.

"Who is talking about killing? We will distribute them their salary and to exhibit to them how good an employer Richard is, they will also get adequate extra money to buy themselves an airline ticket back to the USA. After that, they will be out of our way, and it will be you and me and the Maltese Falcon," Cyrus said, as he placed his head on Samantha breasts and started to fondle her breast. Cyrus and Samantha had been long waiting for this moment. At present, they had their desires, but they seemed unsettled. They did not know how to handle the state of affairs that they brought themselves into. Suddenly, they had authority over a huge amount of money and not to include the worth of the Maltese Falcon. They had never had been accountable over their lives. Richard had them under his power and he determined what they would do. Now with Richard out of the picture, they had no concept how to manage on their own.

Jason and Rita were desperately struggling to make their way out. It was dark and slippery; they could barely see each other's face in the darkness inside the narrow passage. Midway through the passage, Jason stepped on a wet, slippery rock and twisted his ankle.

He was in real pain, and he could hardly put any pressure on his ankle. Rita kept repeatedly insisting that they should stop and rest, but Jason declined. The pain did not stop him from dragging himself out of that hell hole passage.

Eventually, they sighted sunlight in the far distance. They knew for certain that they were only minutes away from their time to get their vengeance. The nearer they got to the end, the brighter and cooler it got. They could hear the voices of the tour guides and the sounds of the motor boats.

"We made it; we are almost there," said Rita with joy.

Finally, they obtained what they worked hard for; they reached the end of the passage and into the main cave. Jason, with Rita's help, managed to crawl against a huge rock to rest. Jason was in tremendous pain, and he knew that he had to get out of that cave. Rita was feeling sorry for Jason, and she examined his ankle. There was a lot of swelling around Jason's ankle, and she tried to call for help. Jason hurriedly covered Rita's mouth and told her to be quiet. He notified Rita that if she asked for help, then they would have to explain how they got there and what they were doing in the cave. Rita sat down beside Jason.

"Rita, we have to split up now," Jason told her.

"What do you mean?" questioned Rita timidly.

"What I honestly mean is that you go and give your father a reasonable early warning. Tell him that he had better to be off this island before I catch up with him, because once I do, they will all be dead, that goes for you too, if you get into my way," Jason told Rita in a treating manner.

"No, I am not going to leave you on your own, moreover, did they give us a fair warning of what they were going to do to us?" Rita replied, uneasy. "If my father has got something to do with this merciless plan to leave us up in that cave to die, then he certainly deserves to die also; I am pissed and angry. I am hungry and filthy. Look at me. I have never been so embarrassed in my life. This was supposed to be a vacation, not a race with death."

At this moment, Rita was absolutely furious, and she could not care less what happened to her father when Jason caught up with him.

Jason now realized that Rita was really angry; he gave her a hug, and told her to keep her voice down. "Now, let's get out of here," Rita proposed to Jason.

"Here is what we ought to do," Jason started to say. "We wait until there are no tour boats in the cave, and then we jump into the water, and we'll wait until the next tour boat comes."

"What shall we tell them if they ask us what happened and why we are in the cave swimming?" questioned Rita.

"We'll tell them that we were in a rubber boat, and that it got pricked against the rocks, and it has sunk," replied Jason.

"Do you know that you have a criminal mind?" expressed Rita, smiling.

"When you are dealing with criminals, you have to think like one," Jason answered.

They did just what they had planned. Rita jumped into the water first and Jason slowly made it to the edge of the rocks and jumped in. Both were counting the minutes, awaiting the next tour boat to come to the cave. Jason could barely tread water because of his aching ankle. Rita was enjoying the cool salt water, and she splashed Jason to have some fun. As they were splashing each other, they heard the voice of a tour guide close by. They got nearer to each other and pretended that they were exhausted from swimming.

As soon as the tour boat entered into the cave, Jason and Rita started yelling for help. The tour guide was in a state of shock when he saw the two of them swimming inside the cave. He quickly threw them a life jacket. "You are crazy Americans; you can't swim in here. Wait for me. I'll go get help," said the tour guide as he turned the boat around. It was not long after he left, he returned with an empty boat.

As he entered into the cave, he mumbled to himself. "There is something going on here." The tour guide got the boat closer to Jason and Rita, and helped them to get into the boat. "What happened? Why are you in the cave swimming?" he questioned. He continued to tell them that the current inside the caves was very dangerous, and that they could have drowned. Later, he asked them how they got inside the cave.

Jason and Rita looked at each other and Rita signaled to Jason to say something, "Oh, we came with a small rubber boat, and it rubbed against the rocks, got punctured, and it sank," said Jason, smiling.

Coming out of the cave, Jason looked around, and he did not see Richard's yacht. He looked at Rita and said, "It appears that we have got lots of work to do."

Jason asked the tour guide if he had seen a big yacht anchored outside the cave entrance.

"Yes, a big yacht was anchored outside the cave for two days and then left. Later in the afternoon, the yacht returned and anchored again. One man went inside the cave in small motor boat and came out with a woman with him. Then they left with the yacht," finished saying the guide with a little understanding of English.

"It doesn't make good sense," Jason told Rita. The tour guide took them to shore, and Jason thanked him. Before they separated, Jason asked the guide for his name and promised him that he will be back to compensate him for his help.

Jason and Rita walked up the hill slowly as Jason had a tough time waking with his tender ankle. As soon as they reached the top of the hill, Jason waved down a taxi. The taxi driver wasn't too satisfied to have them riding in his taxi soaked and wet. Jason gave the driver the name of the hotel where he had checked during the day they arrived in Malta.

"Where are we going?" asked Rita softly.

"To my hotel," replied Jason. "You see, when we arrived in Malta, I checked in this hotel because I didn't want to stay on your father's yacht. I desired a place to hide the money that your father gave me, and I had bad feelings all along about Cyrus, especially when he started to be very friendly with me."

It was approximately an hour's long drive to the hotel; Rita and Jason were really worn-out and slept in the back seat of the taxi all the way to the hotel.

"Here we are, sir," said the taxi driver as he woke Jason.

Jason opened his eyes and woke Rita, "Wake up sleepy head." Jason tapped her on the shoulders.

Jason asked the driver to remain there until he got into his room and got the money to pay him. Jason hopped all the way to his room, but he realized that he did not have the keys to his room on him; he had left them on the yacht. He went to the front desk and asked for second key. Jason was questioned by the clerk what happened to the other key; Jason looked at the clerk and said to him, "Look at me, what do you presume happened? I tell you what happened; I got robbed by one of your fellow citizens. Now, are you happy?" Jason made a big situation in the lobby, and he made the clerk and the rest of the workers uncomfortable as he kept criticizing the behaviour of the locals towards the tourist. He made the hotel staff feel remorseful for him, and the clerk gave Jason a new key without asking any more questions. Jason went into his room got the money and went downstairs to pay the driver.

Jason and Rita walked slowly up the stairs to Jason's room and as soon as Jason opened the door, Rita entered the room and she stepped out onto the balcony.

"This is an extremely beautiful view," she said, looking around the attractive view of St. Paul's Bay.

"Never mind the view, we have lots of work to do," replied Jason. "Go and take a quick shower and put these clothes on." Jason gave Rita one of his t-shirts since she didn't have any other clean clothes. Rita took a shower and Jason showered right after her.

As soon as he was done showering, Jason called for room service and ordered a big supper for both since they had nothing to eat for two days. "You have to get some new clothes," Jason told Rita.

"Do you expect me to go shopping with this shirt on only?" Rita asked, embarrassed.

"If you think that I am going to buy your clothes for you by myself, you are nuts. If you do not come with me, then you will have to stay with that shirt," Jason replied.

"Okay, I can put these back on once they dry." Rita picked up her old clothes and hung them on the balcony to dry. "Can we go shopping tomorrow? I am very tired," Rita begged Jason.

"I suppose so, but every minute that passes, they will be slipping away from us and will make it that much harder to find them," replied Jason.

"I don't think so. They think that we are still up in that cave and probably dead by now. Knowing my dad, from what I have seen from him and the other two, they are almost certain that they are enjoying themselves," said Rita.

"Maybe you are right!" Jason replied.

"Lucky you, there are two beds," said Jason.

"What do you mean lucky me?" asked Rita as she jumped onto one of the beds.

"Because if there was only one bed, I would have slept in it, and you would have to sleep on the floor," smiled Jason.

Rita smiled and threw a pillow at Jason, and he threw it back at her.

"Have a good sleep," said Rita. "You too, we are going to need it," replied Jason.

Back at the marina the crew of the *Slik* was anxiously waiting ashore for Richard; it was payday. Cyrus called them on board and asked everyone to sit down.

"Richard authorized me to give you some bad news. He's determined to stay in Malta for a length of time. With your pay, you will find additional cash to buy yourselves an airfare ticket back to the USA. He gave you some supplementary spending money also," said Cyrus while he handed out to the crew their pay and their passports.

"Where is the boss?" asked the captain.

"He is searching for a house to buy," replied Cyrus.

"How is he going to sail back to America?" the captain asked, again mistrustful.

"I don't know. You have to ask him when he returns. You are welcome to wait for him to return and if not I'll ask you to leave, I have work to do," said Cyrus, trying to get rid of the crew fast.

"When do we have to leave Malta?" asked one of the crew members.

"I spoke to the customs' office, and I asked them the same question, they informed me that since you entered Malta as workers and not tourists, you have forty-eight hours to leave the island because you don't have any work permits to stay in Malta."

The captain and the rest of the crew could not comprehend what was going on. They had worked hard for Richard for over five years. The captain and his crew went to their cabins and packed their personal belongings.

Cyrus took a deep breath and called Samantha to come out from where she was hiding. She was worried that the crew would not collaborate with what Cyrus had to tell them, and they might revolt. Cyrus opened the Maltese map and pointed to a small island named Comino.

"We'll go and anchor here." Cyrus pointed to the tiny island on the map. "I will have to call some of my links; I know one that lives in England, and he might be interested in the Falcon. He was a friend of Richard until Richard double-crossed him years ago. I will bet you that he will be more than happy when I tell what happened to my boss."

Samantha asked Cyrus if the contact of his could be trusted. "After what Richard did to him, he might pay double for the Falcon," Cyrus replied.

"Why are we hiding; why on that island?" Samantha asked.

"At this moment I want to be cautious. Besides, this marina is too busy," replied Cyrus. "Now, quit asking so many questions." Cyrus started the engine and sailed to Comino Island.

The morning came by fast for Jason and Rita; they were real tired. They slept over ten hours. The noises of the cars beeping their horns woke Jason up. "It seems I just got to bed," he said to himself as he rolled out of bed while he noticed that Rita was still sleeping.

Jason looked at the wristwatch, and he could not believe what time it was and woke Rita up.

"What time is it?" Rita asked while pulling the bed sheets over her head.

"It's ten o'clock, wake up," said Jason while he rushed to take a shower. After he showered, Jason went to wake up Rita once more as she proceeded back to sleep while Jason was showering. Rita came out of the shower with a towel wrapped around her.

"Boy, I needed that," she said. "I guess I have to wear my old rags again. When are we going shopping for some outfits?" she asked as Rita walked to the balcony to get her clothes where she left them to dry. Rita got dressed and then suddenly she yelled. "Shit! I do not have any money. Everything is on the yacht."

"Don't worry, I will loan you some. With interest of course," Jason informed Rita with a grin on his face. The two of them quickly walked out of the hotel, and Jason requested Rita to wait for him at the hotel lobby.

"Where are you going?" Rita inquired.

"I am going to get the car," Jason replied and continued to walk to the hotel underground parking garage.

Rita stood still like a statue. "He's got a car? How did he manage to arrange all this?"

Jason drove around and stopped in front of the hotel where he left Rita waiting. She got into the car and asked Jason, "Where did you get this? What are you, some kind of a secret agent?" She could not figure out how Jason prearranged all of the accommodations.

"In Malta, when you show some cash, everybody becomes your friend, and I made lots of friends in Malta," Jason replied, with a smile on upon his face.

Driving down the busy streets of Malta, Rita was astonished how full of activity the little island could be. It was a hot, sunny morning, and Jason got thirsty; he asked Rita if she wanted something to drink prior to her shopping.

"Yes, that would be likeable. A cold beer would hit the spot at this moment," replied Rita.

Jason parked the car as they walked alongside the shoreline to an outdoor bar. Indeed, the cold beer comforted their thirst. After they finished their drinks, Jason decided to show Rita around the village of Bugibba. Walking along the busy, crowded street Rita saw a women's clothing store and she told Jason that she would like to take look inside the store. While Rita was inside the clothing store, Jason stood outside waiting for her.

Chapter 23
Body Discovered

Next door to the casual clothing store there was a souvenir shop, and to kill some time Jason walked inside to look around, and at the same time to enjoy the cool of the store air condition. He did not see anything, in particular, that he was interested in, and decided to purchase the daily Maltese newspaper. He went outside and sat on a shady bench under a tree. Jason calmly opened the newspaper, looked at the front page and read the headline. "Dead man's body found at sea," written in bold letters.

At the moment he started reading the article, Rita came out from the clothing store and told Jason that she was finished shopping for the day. Jason enfolded the newspaper and asked Rita, "Did you purchase sufficient clothing with my money?" As he glanced at the four bags of clothing that she was carrying. "We can't go around with all these bags." Jason notified Rita.

"What do you suggest?" questioned Rita.

"We'll take them back to the hotel, and at the same time you can change into a new and clean outfit that you purchased with my money," said Jason smiling.

They arrived at the hotel; Rita got out of the car and asked Jason, "Aren't you going to help carrying these bags to the room?"

"They aren't my clothes, I just paid for them," he replied, and he waved at her.

Rita told Jason that he doesn't have to keep reminding her that he paid for her new clothing. She stepped out from the car, picked up the bags and walked towards the hotel entrance. Jason sat in the car, and he reached into the back seat for the newspaper. He started to read the article and unexpectedly he stopped reading. He read the article and with great astonishment and said to himself, "Oh my God, they killed him."

Jason didn't know exactly what to do and in what manner he was going to give Rita the bad news. He stepped out of the car and ran up to the room. He opened the door and bumped into Rita as she was on her way out the door.

"Now you come! I don't need your help at the moment," she said as she shoved Jason out of her way. Jason did not say a word. He stood at the doorway silent.

"Are you alright? Is there something wrong because you look like you have seen a ghost," asked Rita. Jason entered the room and requested Rita to step inside.

With a puzzled look, she entered the room and closed the door behind her. "I think you better sit down," Jason asked Rita.

"What is wrong?" she asked again.

"I don't have to kill your father after all," he told her in a tranquil voice.

"What are you talking about?" she asked.

"Your father had nothing to do with what Cyrus did to us," he replied.

Rita slowly stood up from the chair. "Oh, is my father here?" She ran to the balcony to look outside. She went back inside, sat down beside Jason on the bed, and she asked, "Where is he? Have you seen him?"

"I'm sorry I have some remorseful news. They found your father's dead body in the sea not far from where we were at the cave. The newspaper article reads that he was stabbed several times," Jason expressed with sadness.

Rita started to cry. "How do you know this?" she asked with tears in her eyes.

"It's in this newspaper," he said, as he wiped Rita's tears from her face.

"Those two, they had it all planned out," she said. "We have to find them."

"Don't worry, we will. Now we have to go to the police and tell them everything," said Jason calmly.

"But we will be in trouble," cried out Rita.

"We have no choice. We have to go to the authorities and take our chances. Besides, we have to give your dad a decent burial," replied Jason.

They went back to the car and drove away to the police station. As soon they walked in, Jason asked one of the police officers at the front desk to speak to somebody.

"What do you want?" asked the police officer.

"I have some information about this man's murder," said Jason as he showed the officer the newspaper article.

"I will take you to the police chief Inspector in command of this murder. Follow me," the police officer led them to the chief Inspector's office. The officer asked Rita and Jason to wait outside the chief's door as he went inside the office to speak to the chief Inspector. After a short moment, the officer came out and told Rita and Jason that the Inspector would see them. Jason told the Inspector the whole story, including the finding of the Maltese Falcon. "So, you are saying that this couple attempted to kill you too, so they could keep the treasure for themselves. That treasure belongs to the Maltese government, and nobody is going to leave Malta with it!" the Inspector shouted.

He ordered to have the island patrolled by the coast guard. He instructed them to keep an eye on the yacht *Slik* and to apprehend anyone seen on it with caution because they could be armed and dangerous. "Do you have any pictures of this couple of Cyrus and Samantha?" he inquired.

"No, we don't, everything we have is on the yacht," answered Jason.

"And you," aiming at Jason, "where did you get the money to buy her clothes and to pay for the hotel since you left all your belongings on the yacht?" the Inspector interrogated Jason.

"That is my money that I brought with me from the USA," Jason replied.

"Thank you. You can leave now, but don't leave the island," ordered the Inspector.

"Inspector, our passports are also on the yacht. If you don't find them, Rita and I will need new passports," Jason told to the chief Inspector.

"Don't worry. Malta is small, and if they are still here, we will find them. Besides, you are also suspects, and you don't need any passports until we find out the truth," replied the Inspector.

Rita and Jason left the police station, and they got to the car. "We have to find them before the police do, or we can kiss that statue bye-bye," Jason said while starting the car.

Jason had no thought about where he was to start looking for Cyrus and Samantha, and he kept driving along the shoreline hoping that he would see the yacht anchored somewhere. Jason observed that they were being tailed by another car. "Whatever, you don't look back; I think we have company. We are being pursued," Jason informed Rita.

"Who is following us?" Rita asked fearfully.

"I think it's the police. It is going to be very complicated to do anything with them following us," said Jason.

"Can't you lose them?" Rita asked Jason.

"Not now, but I will later." Jason kept driving. He frequently stopped at different locations to make certain that the car that was following them since they left the police station was indeed following them. "There is only one way to lose them, run them out of gas," Jason commented. He stopped at a gas station and filled the car gas tank. He noted the car that was following them stopped at a near distance also, but did not fill up the gas tank. Jason took that opportunity to take Rita for a sightseeing ride around the island. Shortly after they left the gas station, he looked at the rear-view mirror and noticed that the car that was pursuing them started to slow down. "Well, I think they finally ran out of gas," said Jason laughing.

"You are an evil spirit. I told you that you had a criminal mind. I would not in my life think about your crazy ideas," said Rita with a smile. They were in the countryside and there were no gas stations around for miles, only farmland.

"Now we are on our own. I have to find an old friend of mine." Jason had many friends when he lived in Malta; he anticipated that they would still remember him. He pulled in front of a bar and parked the car.

"Is this a friend of yours?" Rita asked.

"Yes, a very good friend," replied Jason. They walked in, and Jason approached the bartender. Jason recognized the man behind the bar and said to himself, "Yes, that's him alright." Jason and Rita sat down at the bar lounge, and the bartender asked them what they would like to drink.

Jason spoke in Maltese and ordered his favourite drink, the only drink that his old friend can make, because he produced it himself. "Give me *zonqra*," which means a piece of limestone.

The barman stared at Jason in bewilderment and said in a loud voice, "Jason, is that you?"

"Yes, it is me, Edgar," Jason said as they embraced each other. Jason introduced Rita to Edgar as his girlfriend. Edgar did not know how to speak any English, so while Jason and Edgar talked of the past, Rita just sat quietly, not understanding a word the two old friends were saying.

"Now what brings you back to Malta?" Edgar asked Jason.

"Business," Jason replied.

"Business, what type of business are you in nowadays?" Edgar asked.

Jason did not know what to say, and quickly he replied, "I'm in the real estate business. I came to Malta to take samples of the limestone to take them back to America for a big developer who wants to build a hotel here in Malta."

Edgar, not wise to know any better, believed Jason and wished him much success in the business.

"Edgar, I need a favour," Jason asked.

"Sure, old friend, and what sort of a favour?" Edgar asked.

"I need a gun, some ammunition, and some explosives," replied Jason.

"What does a real estate business man want a gun for? Explosives I will understand. Tell me, my old friend, are you in some kind of trouble?" curiously, Edgar asked.

Jason told his friend that indeed he was in big trouble, but he didn't want Edgar to get engaged in Jason's problems. Edgar shrugged his shoulders and told Jason, "Well, my friend, you came to the right place. Follow me," replied Edgar.

The three of them walked toward the back room was Edgar had a secret room to hide all types of supplies he bought from contrabands.

Edgar opened a large trunk and said, "Take your pick, old friend."

Jason looked inside the trunk and could not believe his eyes the amount of stock of ammunitions that were stored in the trunk. "You've even got hand grenades! What are you planning to do, start an army to take over Malta?" slowly replied Jason with a laugh.

"You don't think I can make a living by selling beer only, do you?" Edgar replied.

"You haven't changed a bit," Jason replied.

Jason leaned against the wall; he started to visualize the horrified ordeal that he and Rita went through after Cyrus left them abandoned inside the cave. Edgar looked at him and told Jason that whatever trouble he was in, he must have been personified by the way Jason was looking at the ammunition.

Jason walked to the trunk and picked up a gun and two-hand grenades. "That's all I need. Thank you, friend, I have to go now, and I will see you soon." Both friends shook hands.

"Yes, we'll see you later, friend," Edgar told Jason.

After they stepped outside Edgar's bar, Rita broke her silence and apprehensively asked Jason, "What do you require the hand grenades for?"

"If I can't get them, then I'll blow them," replied Jason. "It's getting late, let's go and get some sleep. Tomorrow we are going for a cruise around the islands," Jason responded, as he carefully stored the hand grenades and the gun under the driver seat.

"What islands?" softly asked Rita astonished.

"They call them the Maltese Islands, because there are three islands, Gozo, Comino, and Malta. If they are in Malta, they have to be on the yacht. When we locate the yacht, we will definitely hit upon them too," Jason replied. For Jason, killing Cyrus and Samantha's forecasting was the only revenge.

Chapter 24
Cyrus' Contact

Cyrus and Samantha anchored the yacht in a little harbour outside the blue lagoon bay in Comino. They could not get closer to the shore because of the shallow water, and they had to use the small motor boat to come to land. Once they arrived on shore, they walked towards the hotel that Cyrus's informer instructed him to go to. They could not overlook the hotel, because it was the only hotel on the relatively tiny island. As they arrived in the hotel, Cyrus asked the security guard that he have an appointment with the hotel manager.

"Who shall I say you are?" politely asked the security guard.

"My name is Cyrus," he replied.

"Yes, we were notified that you were coming. Please wait over here and I will tell Mr. Godfrey that you have arrived."

Cyrus looked at the reservation book at the hotel lobby and noticed that the hotel had no guests registered, he got tense.

The security guard left Cyrus and Samantha in the room as he proceeded to inform Mr. Godfrey that his guests had arrived. Cyrus was extremely uneasy and told Samantha that he was seriously concerned about the arrangement and that perhaps they ought to leave. Samantha discouraged Cyrus from leaving.

After a very short while the guard returned and notified Cyrus and Samantha told them that Mr. Godfrey would be there momentarily.

Samantha strolled out of the room and moved outside and sat on a bench. She observed, and she wondered why there was a hotel on this tiny island when there were no tourists. She could hear loud voices from the distance but the voices she heard were coming from the beach, far distance from the hotel.

Strangely, she walked back inside. "Why are there no people on this island?" Samantha asked Cyrus. "There are no roads or cars on this island, so in what manner does a person get around?"

"I don't know. Do I look like a history professor?" answered Cyrus.

There was knocking at the door, and Mr. Godfrey walked into the room. "Oh. Mister Cyrus. John related me everything about you," expressed Mr. Godfrey.

"Where is John?" asked Cyrus calmly.

"He couldn't make the trip. John has additional business in Holland to take attention of. He ought to be back in a few days. Do you wish to wait until his return to conduct business?" questioned Mr. Godfrey.

"Who is in command?" asked Samantha in a brave tone of voice.

"I am. Where is your expensive statue?" asked Mr. Godfrey.

"I have it on the yacht. I couldn't transport it with us; first of all, it's quite heavy to carry, and secondly I had to anchor outside the bay because of the shallow water," replied Cyrus.

Godfrey stepped outside the door to take a better look at Samantha and asked Cyrus if he had ever seen such extremely beautiful, calm azure water. Cyrus started getting agitated and told Godfrey that actually he did see beautiful azure water before when he was in Hawaii. Cyrus strongly insisted to talk about business and not about blue waters. Godfrey turned towards Cyrus and told him that he needed to relax, and then he asked, "You mean to tell me that among the two of you couldn't carry this golden statue?"

"Do you realize how heavy that sucker is? We would never be able to carry it all the way up here by ourselves. You will have to come on the yacht yourself to view it," Cyrus recommended.

"When do you want me to examine it?" asked Godfrey fully realized that Cyrus was getting panicky.

"Give me five days and I will remain in touch with you," replied Cyrus while he rushed towards the door.

"That is fine with me, but why wait five days? I can come now," suggested Godfrey.

"Just give me five days, alright?" yelled Cyrus from outside the door as he hurried down the path.

"Okay, don't get angry. Don't forget you need me," said Godfrey with a smile.

Samantha and Cyrus followed the rugged path from the hotel to the shore were they had left the motor boat. Going down the path Samantha asked, "Why wait five days? We may well be out of here in five days."

"I don't trust that man," replied Cyrus. "John never mentioned anything about Godfrey. He told me he would be here himself," Cyrus said while he stopped.

Samantha asked, "Now, what are we going to do?"

"First, we have to change the name of the yacht, then we have to hide the bird statue on land, somewhere safe," Cyrus finished saying as he continued to walk to the motor boat.

Samantha got worried with Cyrus's behaviour and at that moment she had no idea what Cyrus just told her. Perhaps she should go to see Godfrey and make a deal with him herself, and terminate Cyrus. These thoughts ran through her head.

Suddenly, she stopped and yelled at Cyrus, "You never give me straight answers, and you at no time plan in advance. You always wait for the last minutes to take decisions. Now tell again why we need to hide the Falcon statue?"

Cyrus was really surprised to hear Samantha talk to him in that manner. Calmly, he replied, "Just in case he tries to steal it from us."

"You mean Godfrey?" softly asked Samantha again.

"Yes, we have to find a good location where we can hide the statue on land," replied Cyrus.

"Why do we have to change the yacht's name?" asked Samantha with a confused look on her face.

"Samantha, please don't ask me any further questions," replied Cyrus. They got into the motor boat and cruised around the small island looking for a safe place to hide the golden statue of the Maltese Falcon. When they returned to the yacht, Cyrus told Samantha that they had to anchor at another location somewhere they could not be seen from the hotel.

They cruised around the tiny island twice just to confuse Mr. Godfrey, who was observing Cyrus's moves from his hotel window. Finally, Cyrus found what he thought would be a good area to anchor. He rushed down to the supply room and grabbed a can of paint and some paintbrushes. Cyrus was very nervous and kept pacing back and forth on the deck; he had no idea what to do. He threw the paintbrushes and a can of paint in the motor boat, and then he jumped into the water and pulled behind him the motor boat. Samantha was getting easily upset with Cyrus's actions; she leaned over the deck railing and asked Cyrus, "Where are you going? And what are you doing with the paint?"

"I have already told you not to ask me any more stupid questions," replied Cyrus.

He eventually changed the name of the yacht from *Slik* to *Lick*. Cyrus made his way up on deck, and he asked Samantha to help him to lower the statue into the motorboat and slowly manoeuvre to shore.

They carried the statue using Jason's idea by transporting it on a stretcher. Cyrus obscured the statue under a pile of rocks and marked the site with a letter "S" on top. Samantha kept insisting not to wait five days to contact Godfrey and related to Cyrus that the sooner they arranged the deal the earlier they would have the money. For once, Cyrus agreed with Samantha.

Chapter 25
The Deal

The day after, Cyrus called Godfrey and gave him the particulars where the yacht was anchored. Godfrey appeared at the yacht, and gave a suspicious look to Cyrus and asked Cyrus why he had moved to a different location. Cyrus straightforward told him that he wanted more privacy as he looked at Samantha with a smile. Godfrey did not believe whatever thing that Cyrus had said to him, and he was getting annoyed with Cyrus's double talk. "I noticed that you have changed the name of your yacht. That could get you in a lot of trouble with the port authorities," Godfrey warned Cyrus.

"Yeah, so?" replied Cyrus with an ignorant tone of voice.

"Okay, let's see what you have," said Godfrey.

"We will have to go to shore," Cyrus, said nervously. He was getting very uncomfortable around Godfrey. They went to the location where Cyrus hid the statue, took the rocks from around the statue. "There is the baby," said Cyrus.

"Oh my god. It isn't that a beauty," said Godfrey, while kneeling down to take a closer look. "So you want five hundred million American dollars for this?" he asked.

"Yes. No more, no less," replied Cyrus, looking straight at Godfrey.

"I'll give you twenty million. No more, no less," smiled Godfrey.

Cyrus looked at Samantha, and she gave him good indication to say yes.

Cyrus simply ignored her and yelled, "Twenty million dollars? Are you out of your mind? Forget it, I'll go somewhere else." Cyrus started to hide the statue back.

"Mr. Cyrus, how faraway do you think you can go, and where can you go? The Maltese law enforcement is searching for this yacht. The police, as well, found the dead body of the yacht's possessor. They said that he was stabbed several times, that's a murder and in Malta that's a lifetime in prison. At present, a good reward would be awarded for any information that will lead to the capture of the killer," said Godfrey as he winked at Samantha.

Samantha asked, "How do they know about the yacht?"

"They found the registration papers on the dead body when was recovered," replied Godfrey, as he turned and looked at Cyrus, stepped towards him stopping inches away from Cyrus's face. Godfrey was so close to Cyrus that he could smell the odour of sweat dripping down Cyrus's face. "I don't have to make any offers to you. I can just kill right here, now, and collect the reward money and take the Falcon for free. I am like you; I am a criminal, and that's how it is. Take or leave it." Godfrey turned around and walked towards Samantha, looked at her breasts, and said to her, "I wouldn't kill you. I can use a sexy woman like you." Godfrey turned back and asked Cyrus to make up his mind fast.

"Okay then, I have no choice but to accept your offer. Okay, it's a deal," Cyrus, replied with a trembling voice.

"I require at least three days to obtaining all that cash, and by the way, you ought to figure out how you'll hide twenty million dollars from the airport customs. For a small fee, I can transfer the money to any bank in the world for you," said Godfrey.

"We'll wait. You know where to find us," replied Cyrus. Godfrey shook Cyrus's hand and told him that he would be back in three days with the cash.

Godfrey got to his boat and left Cyrus and Samantha on the beach bewildered.

Samantha asked Cyrus, "I thought you said that you don't trust that man Godfrey?"

"I don't, and you have seen why. I had an awful taste about him the minute I saw him. Besides, we do not have any other alternatives. You heard what he said that the authorities are looking for us. We have to close this deal fast so we can get the hell out of here," replied Cyrus. "Now help me to hide the statue at a different location."

Back on the mainland, Jason and Rita were ready to get on board the cruise boat, when they were denied boarding by a police officer, and told that they had to wait ashore. The police officer phoned the Inspector at the police depot to notify the Inspector that he had the two suspects. "I am sorry but you can't go on this boat," said the police officer to Jason.

"Why not?" We paid for the tickets," replied Jason.

"All I can tell you is that you two have to wait and that you can't board. That is the order from my Inspector," answered the police officer.

"What are we supposed to do with these tickets?" inquired Jason.

"You can use them for the next cruise that leaves in an hour," replied the police officer. It took the Inspector about twenty minutes to get to the dock where the cruise boats anchored.

As soon as the Inspector saw Jason, he told him with a smiling face, "You are a very smart man, Mr. Jason."

"Well, thank you, but what are you talking about?" questioned Jason.

"That was very smart of you. You played a very dirty trick on my constables when you left them abandoned in the countryside," said the Inspector.

Jason was pretending that he didn't have a clue what the Inspector was talking about and said to the Inspector, "Did you have us followed? If you did, then it wasn't my fault. I was showing Rita the beautiful countryside of your sunny island. Besides, why were we being followed?" asked Jason.

"Everyone is a suspect, including you two," the Inspector replied.

"Suspects of what? You wouldn't think that I would kill my own father now, would you?" Rita asked in heatedly voice.

"You say he is your father, but you don't have any proof of that. You said that you were American, and you don't have proof of that either," responded the Inspector. "So, you are going for a cruise around Malta?"

"Yes, we are here on vacation, do you remember?" said Jason, who started to get mad at the Inspector's delay tactics.

"So you desire to go for a cruise. Yes, you can go, but I am coming with you, and I will be your tour guide. Let's go," said the Inspector as he led them on board the cruise boat. They boarded the cruise ship, and the Inspector said, "You know, I have never been on one of these cruises. I will come with you and keep you company."

Jason looked at Rita and smiled and whispered into her ear, "You know how roasting he is going to get wearing that uniform in this hot sun all day and in this heat?"

Once the cruise ship left the harbour, all the decks were covered with the hot sun. The passengers on deck began to take off their shirts. Jason and Rita walked across the deck with their bathing suits on.

The Inspector was trying to find a shaded place to stay under, but he did not want to lose sight of the two suspects. It was not long after when the Inspector approached Jason and asked him, "Do you have to remain under the sun?" It has been over two hours since we left, and it is too hot," said the Inspector with sweat pouring down his head. His police uniform was drenched with sweat.

"We are here on holiday in Malta for the sun, and this is a cruise boat," replied Jason.

"Alright, alright. You are a very bad person, Jason. I am going to find a shady location where I can feel the breeze," said the Inspector, wiping the sweat off his forehead, and he went down to the lower deck. The cruise guide announced that they would be docking in Comino soon.

As the cruise ship got closer to Comino Island, Jason looked straight ahead at all the boats and yachts anchored in the bay. There was one thing that caught his eye, a yacht that was anchored far out of the bay. "That is curious. Why would that yacht be anchored out there and not in the bay?" Jason said to himself.

As the cruise ship got nearer to the dock, Jason kept looking at the yacht. The closer they got; the more anxious Jason came to be. "That yacht looks familiar," Jason told Rita. "I'll be damned. They say that you can run but you can't hide. Malta is small but Comino is even smaller," said Jason. "You can run, but you can't hide, Cyrus," said Jason as the cruise ship sailed close by the yacht. Jason could see Cyrus and Samantha sunbathing on the *Slik* deck. "I told your father that Cyrus was not an extremely smart man."

"Well, you two look like you have seen a ghost, or should I say, former partners?" approaching from behind them said the Inspector.

"You know about them?" asked Jason.

"Yes, of course. I received a call from the coast guard department reporting that this yacht has been anchored in this bay for three days now. The yacht name didn't match their entry records. They ran a check on the name, and it almost matches the name you gave me," said the Inspector wiping off the sweat from his face.

"Okay, now what are you going to do?" Rita asked the Inspector.

"What do you want me to do?" acknowledged the Inspector. "Arrest them?"

"Yes, of course," replied Rita. "They killed my father, and they tried to kill us. Not to mention, they are in possession of a treasure that belongs to Malta."

"So far, we don't have any evidence that they killed your father, or that they have the Maltese Falcon," responded the Inspector.

"The Inspector is right. There is no evidence," replied Jason.

"That's right. I knew you were a very smart man," replied the Inspector.

"There must be something we can do," asked Rita.

"Mr. Jason is smart, let him come up with a plan."

As soon as the cruise ship docked in Comino, Jason, Rita, and the Inspector went ashore to the Inspector's relief. Jason called the Inspector and said to him to go with them. "Come on, police Inspector; let me buy you a nice, cold drink."

"That is a very good idea. I am so thirsty; I could drink a gallon of water right now," said the Inspector with a smile upon his face.

Jason put one arm on the Inspector's shoulder. As they started to walk he said, "You are a good policeman, but you are a lousy dresser. You knew that we were going on the cruise ship, why did not you change from that uniform and wear some light clothing?"

"I am not smart like you, Mr. Jason," slowly replied the Inspector.

Arriving at the bar, Jason ordered three chilled beers. The Inspector refused to drink the beer and asked for a cold cola instead. The Inspector told Jason that he was not supposed to drink any alcoholic beverage while he was on duty. With the Inspector tagging along it would be more difficult to get at Cyrus, and Jason decided to make a deal with the Inspector.

Jason told the Inspector, "Inspector, all you want is the treasure, and all we want is revenge."

"I know what I want," responded the Inspector. "I want the Falcon to stay in Malta where it belongs with the Maltese people, and I want a promotion."

Jason and Rita were getting amused with the Inspector's humour. Jason, smiling at the Inspector, said, "Alright then, this is the deal. We help you get the treasure, and you help us to get our money and the passports from the yacht."

"That is easy and it sounds like a fair deal to me," replied the Inspector, "But how?"

"I have a plan," said Jason.

"Okay, tell me. However, please let's go in the shade," begged the Inspector.

Rita and Jason laughed and the three of them went to sit under a shady tree. Jason told the Inspector his plan, the three of them agreed.

"All you have to do is to make sure they don't leave the island. I need two days to get everything together. When it's over you will be the most popular man in Malta, and you might even get that promotion you have been waiting for," said Jason.

It was a nine hour cruise around the Maltese islands, and the Inspector was exhausted.

When they returned at the dock in Malta, the Inspector could not wait for the ship to dock. He approached Jason. "Mr. Jason. I believe in you and I trust you, so please do not initiate any problems. Let's work together on this case. I will help you if you help me," begged the Inspector.

"You have my word," replied Jason as he shook hands with the Inspector. "I'll see you in two days," Jason told the Inspector.

"Yes, no monkey business please, okay?" begged the Inspector while he opened the car door for Rita.

Jason and Rita drove away.

Chapter 26
No trust

The Inspector commanded two police officers to shadow Jason. "This time don't lose them," he yelled. "And keep in contact with me."

Jason's proposal was that the day after, when it got dark, Jason, Rita and the Inspector would go on the island of Comino and steal the statue from Cyrus. At least, that is what Jason told the Inspector the plan was.

The Inspector was acting as a simpleton around Jason and Jason took the bait. After he left the cruise ship, the Inspector rushed home, took a cold shower, and changed into his regular street clothes. He called the police headquarters and requested to have six police officers to escort him. He wanted to get to Comino before Jason and Rita. "If someone comes looking for me, tell them I am out," the Inspector told the desk sergeant at the police headquarters. "I won't be back for two days. This is police business."

The Inspector along the six police officers drove to Mellieha Bay in a police van. A police motor boat was waiting for them to accompany them across the bay to Comino. When they arrived at Comino, the Inspector ordered the police officers to remain tight and not to be noticeable. "All we have to do is wait and stay out of sight," he ordered.

Back at the hotel, Jason told Rita regarding the alteration of the plans. "We'll go tonight," he told her.

"You promised the Inspector that we would go in two days, and that he will be coming with us," Rita replied.

"Never mind what I told him. We are going tonight," Jason insisted.

"How are we going to get to Comino?" Rita asked.

"We will steal a boat from the fishermen harbour," replied Jason.

"What harbour? Jason, I do not like this. Why steal a boat when we can rent one?" appealed Rita.

"We will return it, of course; we'll just borrow one for a limited time," Jason finished saying.

"Put on some dark clothes and the bathing suit," said Jason. Jason pulled the gun from under the mattress and put it in the carry bag.

Jason cautiously wrapped the hand grenades in a towel, and lay by them in the bag along the handgun. Rita was so apprehensive that she was shaking. She stood silently as she watched Jason packing the bag with deadly weapons. She had not for a moment ever thought that she would be implicated in a crime. She wondered how Jason may be so calm, especially when he was the only one that knew what he had planned for Cyrus.

After he finished packing, Jason told Rita that they had to stop at a hardware store to buy a roll of string. Both were quiet as they were driving to the harbour, they did not say a single word all the way. Both were scared, especially Rita. Jason showed no emotions; he stayed composed. He warned Cyrus that he always keeps his promises.

Jason looked at the rear-view mirror, and noticed that they were being followed by another car. He did not try to outrun the car that was following them; he determined to stop at an outdoor bar. He observed that the car that was following them had also stopped some distance away. Once Jason and Rita finished their drinks, they continued the drive to their destination.

The police officers that were following Jason called the Inspector and informed him that Jason was heading north towards Mellieha Bay. The Inspector ordered the police officer to stop the pursuit and to head back to the police headquarters and to wait for additional instructions. The Inspector reorganized the six police officers that were with him on Comino and told them to be ready because Jason was on his way.

"That's strange," said Jason as he noticed that the car that was following then turned around.

"Why, do you think that they stopped following us?" questioned Rita.

Rita was extremely frightened and sat in her seat nervously.

"Maybe they are trying to baffle us, and somebody else determines to follow us. We'll shortly find out," Jason said as he made a u-turn and drove in the opposite direction.

They drove around in the village of Mosta to see if someone was following them. "That's strange; nobody is following us. Let's get back to business," said Jason as he drove towards his destination.

They arrived at the angler's bay; Jason looked around to see if anyone was surveillance them.

"We'll have to wait up until night time. In the meantime, let's pretend that we are sightseeing." Jason took out the camera, and captured photos of the fisherman's boats as they kept walking around the bay until it got dark. Jason and Rita returned to the car; Jason grabbed the bag containing the gun and the hand grenades and walked towards a fishing boat. He threw the bag into the boat and tried to push the boat into the water when suddenly he heard someone approaching. It was one of the fishermen. Jason pulled the bag out of the boat and rapidly, Rita posed by the boat and pretended that Jason was photographing her. When the fisherman got close to them Jason called him over. "Do you have a boat here?" Jason asked the fisherman.

"Yes," responded the fisherman. "Is there something I can do for you?" he asked.

"We would like to go to Comino. How much are you going to charge to take us there?" inquired Jason.

"It is getting dark. Come back tomorrow and I will take you to Comino. Comino is much nicer in daylight, especially the blue lagoon," acknowledged the fisherman as he started to walk away.

"Wait. Please, wait," called Rita. "We have to get to Comino now. My father is waiting for us. It is his birthday and we want to be at his party," Rita told him, hoping that the fisherman would feel sorry for her.

"Alright, alright, sixty euros and I will take you," said the fisherman.

"Thirty euros," replied Jason.

"No," the fisherman said as he turned around.

"Alright, okay. We'll pay you sixty euros," said Rita.

Jason paid the man; they followed the fisherman to his boat. "We have to get there fast, before it gets too dark," Jason told the fisherman.

"Don't worry, you'll be there before sunset," replied the fisherman.

The fisherman took Jason and Rita at a sandy beach on Comino Island. As soon as they reached shallow water, Jason and Rita jumped out of the boat and waved good-bye to the fisherman.

Jason looked around and all he could see in the darkness was the lights of the yacht. He told Rita not to turn the flashlight on and warned her to watch where she was stepping because she could get her feet cut on the rough, sharp rocks. Slowly, and cautiously, they reached the hilltop.

"Look over there, nearby is a bonfire, it must be them," Rita brought to Jason's attention.

"Yeah, the small boat is there too. You wait here; I have something to do by myself first." Jason reached in the bag and pulled out the roll of string, roll of tape and the two-hand grenades. Gently, he went down the hill. Very cautious, he walked towards the beach, and swam towards Cyrus's small motor boat. He taped the two-hand grenades to the back of the boat, and tied the string to the hand grenade pins. Jason unrolled the twine and tied the end of the twine to a big rock. Slowly, he went back to where he had left Rita. "They are going to have a blast off, once they pull out," said Jason.

"I am scared," said Rita.

"Don't chicken on me now. I need you for your father's sake," said Jason, putting back on his clothes.

"Okay, I'll do my best," replied Rita.

"If it makes you feel any better; I am scared as well," said Jason as he gave Rita a hug.

In the meantime, the Inspector was on the opposite side of the hill from where Jason was. He observed Jason swimming towards the small boat, but he couldn't see what Jason was doing.

"What did he go to the boat for?" quietly asked one of the police officers.

"I don't know. Maybe he did something to the motor so it will not start. Just keep an eye on him," ordered the Inspector.

The Inspector knew that Jason was an intelligent person. Therefore, he was wondering what Jason was doing. From where he was hiding, the Inspector could not evaluate what was occurring on the beach around the fire, and requested the other police officers to manoeuvre closer.

Cyrus and Samantha were having a celebration party. With them on the beach were Godfrey and his girlfriend. Jason could observe the four of them from where he was hiding. He kept his composure.

"Who is the other couple?" asked Rita gently.

"I don't know, perhaps the buyer," replied Jason. "Here, keep this in a secure area." Jason handed to Rita a key.

"What is this for?" She asked.

"This is the key to the safety deposit box at the hotel. If something transpires to me, go and get the rest of the money," said Jason with a distraught look on his face.

Rita was in a state of shock; she did not know what to say. She attempted to return the key back to Jason. "I don't want this key; everything will be alright. Besides, I don't have any pockets to put in," she said as she handed the key out to Jason.

"Just put the key in your bra. That is the safest place," replied Jason, smiling. Her hands trembling, Rita grabbed the key, opened her shirt, and tucked the key in her bra.

"We have to get comfortable. We won't be able do anything until daybreak," said Jason as he was trying to rest on his back against a smooth rock, closed his eyes trying to get some sleep.

Rita, seated next to Jason, could not relax either. She was concerned for Jason's well-being and if something should happen to him. She hated the minute when she decided to join her father on this expedition.

"Look, they're leaving," Rita called as she woke up Jason.

Jason slowly opened his eyes and asked, "Who is leaving?"

"The other couple," replied Rita.

Jason pulled his head out from behind the rock; he observed that the other couple that was with Cyrus and Samantha was ready to leave.

In the silence of the night, Godfrey's voice echoed, "I'll be seeing you tomorrow." Godfrey and his girlfriend walked away together.

"Where are they going?" Jason said to himself.

Cyrus and Samantha looked to be drunk, trying to walk on the sand towards the small motor boat. In the meantime, an enormous noise could be heard that scared Jason and Rita. It was the noise of helicopter engines starting.

"What the hell is that?" expressed Jason, looking towards the direction from where the noise was coming and saw a helicopter flying away.

"Let's go back to the yacht and celebrate some more," said Cyrus to Samantha.

They got into the boat, and Cyrus tried to start the motors.

Nevertheless, he could not find the key. "Where is the key?" he asked Samantha.

"You left it in the ignition," replied Samantha.

"Well, we must have dropped either it on the sand or in the water. We will sleep here tonight, and tomorrow I will swim back to the yacht to bring the other key." Cyrus fell into the water when he tried to get out of the boat.

"I think you had too much to drink," said Samantha as she was trying to help Cyrus up on his feet.

"Tomorrow I will drink even more with twenty million dollars," laughed Cyrus. They could hardly walk on the sandy beach, and they kept falling down on the sand.

Chapter 27
Final Revenge

In Rita's memory flashback, she still could picture Samantha's fist in her face; Rita built up sufficient bravery that she kept hassling Jason for them to pay back Cyrus and Samantha for what they did to them and to her father.

"What are we waiting for? Let's go and get them," she strongly told Jason.

"We have to wait until daylight. I want to see the look on their faces before they die," said Jason while loading his gun. "You get some sleep; it will be at least another three hours before daylight."

"Okay, but don't forget to wake me up," said Rita, trying to find a comfortable position. She could not sleep; she got up and went to sit with Jason. Rita lost all of her nerves, and she began to cry. Jason puts his arms around Rita, held her close to him. He told her to stop the crying. Rita asked Jason what he was going to tell the Inspector when he met with them in two days. Jason told her not to worry, and that he would make up some story to tell the Inspector.

The Inspector and the officers were getting tired and sleepy. They took turns on guard waiting for something to happen. Jason didn't close an eye; he kept looking at the sky waiting for the sun to rise.

Cyrus and Samantha fell asleep on the beach where they had fallen surrounded with empty liquor bottles.

The sky was getting brighter as the red sun surfaced from the horizon. Jason looked from behind the rock where he was hiding and noticed that Cyrus and Samantha were motionless in the same position that they fell on the sand the night before.

Jason woke up Rita, "Okay, it's time," he told her. They walked out from behind the rock, and they headed towards Cyrus and Samantha. Jason raised the gun in the air and fired two shots.

Cyrus and Samantha jumped up to their knees. "What was that?" they asked to each other. The shots also woke the Inspector.

"Look back here, you two," said Jason.

Cyrus turned around slowly and with a stunned look on his face said, "Oh no, it's you. How in the hell did you get out of the cave?" questioned Cyrus, as he tried to stand up.

"Don't even try to stand up. Worms crawl, so crawl," said Jason and pointed the gun towards Cyrus. Cyrus went down on his knees again.

"How did you find us?" asked Cyrus. "And how in the hell did you manage to get out of the cave?"

"I told you a long time ago, that this bum has brains," replied Jason.

Samantha sat down on the sand. "You told me that they would never find a way out of the cave," yelled Samantha at Cyrus. "I knew that you were stupid, what are you going to do? Cyrus?" Samantha threw a hand full of sand at Cyrus.

"Shut up, you bitch," shouted Cyrus back at Samantha. Cyrus turned to Jason and asked him, "What are you going to do now that you found us? We have the statue and you have the gun. If you kill us, you will never find the Falcon," said Cyrus with a smile.

"We don't want the statue; all I want is you two. You tried to kill us and you killed Richard," said Jason.

"I had nothing to do with Richard's death. He had left me in the cave while he went on the yacht and killed Richard. I begged him not to," cried Samantha.

Jason walked closer towards Samantha. "I am here for righteousness. The Falcon statue doesn't belong to me, but you two do," said Jason while pointing the gun at Samantha's head.

"Don't shoot me, please! I'll tell you where the Falcon is hidden," begged Samantha.

"Where is it? If you tell me where the Falcon is, I will let you live" Jason told them.

"Don't, Sam, don't say anything. He doesn't have the courage to pull the trigger!" yelled Cyrus.

Samantha, with tears coming down her face and her body shaking, pointed to the direction. "It is behind those rocks, please don't shoot me!" Samantha continued to cry.

"Shut up, shut up, you damn bitch!" Cyrus started yelling at Samantha. "Now he has the statue and us, you fool. Some partner you turned out to be."

Jason asked Rita to go and investigate. Rita walked towards the direction where Samantha pointed. She turned down a couple of rocks and saw the head of the golden bird.

"It is here," she told Jason

"I am a man who keeps his words. I will take the Falcon, and I will not kill you both on one condition. You go back to the yacht and leave Malta as soon as possible and don't let me see you ever again," said Jason.

Samantha got relaxed hearing Jason say that he will not kill them. She ran towards the motor boat. She knew that he was a man of his word. He proved it in the past; she believed him when he said that he would not kill her and Cyrus.

Cyrus stood up and walked towards the motor boat. He got into the boat, and Cyrus remembered that he had lost the key. "We don't have the key."

"Last night you said you were going to swim to the yacht and bring the other key, so swim and get the spare key," said Jason.

"You mean to tell me that you were here all this time?" implored Cyrus with a shocked look on his face.

"Yes, sir, I was over here observing you two all night. I am a charming guy; I could have killed you both while you were passed out. Here, catch," Jason said as he pulled the key from his pocket and threw it to Cyrus.

Cyrus grabbed the key, and said, "I might not come back to Malta, but I'll get even with you some day."

"I doubt it very much," replied Jason. "Now get lost before I change my mind and shoot both of you."

"Let's go on Cyrus, please. Let's go and get out of here," wined Samantha.

Cyrus started the motor boat slowly heading towards the yacht. Meanwhile, the rope that Jason had tied to the hand grenade pins was becoming stiffer. The pins snapped out from the hand grenades and after a second there was a big blow. The boat blew into pieces, and so did Cyrus and Samantha. Jason stood at the edge of the water watching the boat burning.

Back on top of the hill, the Inspector just could not comprehend what was going on and why the motor boat blew up. "Shall we move in now?" requested one of the police officers.

"No, not yet," replied the Inspector.

"However, he simply killed two people," said the second police officer.

"Have you witnessed him murdering them? All I saw was the boat blowing up far off away from where he was positioned on shore. That's about fifty yards apart from him," expressed the Inspector.

As the boat exploded, Rita screamed and ran for cover behind a big rock.

Jason stood resembling a statue, just staring at the motor boat burning. He turned around, turned to Rita, and said to her, "It's over now. Let's go and get the Maltese Falcon."

Jason and Rita extremely cautiously took the rocks off around the statue.

"How are we going to carry it?" inquired Rita.

"We don't have to carry it; that man with the helicopter is alleged to come with the money. Instead of paying Cyrus, he will pay us, and he can have the damn yacht too," said Jason.

"You mean you are going to sell it to him? You don't know how much money he was going to pay Cyrus," asked Rita.

"Do you have a better idea?" replied Jason.

"I do," a voice came from behind them. Jason and Rita looked back. It was the Inspector and the six police officers. "You were well tried to fool me once again," said the Inspector.

Jason didn't know what to say and asked, "How long have you been here?"

"Since last night, and we've seen everything, even the boat blowing up," the Inspector said with a smile.

"It seems that we both obtained what we wanted. You got them, and I have the Maltese Falcon." The Inspector bent down, and handled the golden statue and said, "The Maltese Falcon. Finally, after all these years, it's back with the Maltese people where it belongs."

"That's true, but how are you going to move this statue?" questioned Jason.

"Don't worry, I have sent for some help already," replied the Inspector.

Jason told the Inspector that he wished to talk to him in private, and the Inspector agreed.

They walked some distance away from the rest of the policeman. Jason told the Inspector that he did what he did without telling him considering that he didn't want the Inspector to see what just happened, and since they had a deal between them Jason didn't want the Inspector to get in trouble. "You told your girlfriend that you would sell the statue to the man in the helicopter," the Inspector told Jason.

"Maybe I should tell you this. There is a man supposed to come to buy this statue from Cyrus," said Jason.

"You mean Mr. Godfrey? Well, Mr. Jason, the Maltese Falcon is not for sale," directly replied the Inspector.

"What about us?" Rita asked.

"You two are a pain the neck. The earlier you leave Malta, the sooner I will feel better," answered the Inspector. "Also the yacht stays here in Malta. It is being repossessed by the Maltese government."

"Can we go on board the yacht? We have to get our passports and our belongings," asked Jason.

"Sure, you can," replied the Inspector. "One of the police officers will come along with you while you are in handcuffs."

"Why in handcuffs?" asked Jason.

"In case you want to try any funny business because you like playing tricks with us," echoed the Inspector, smiling.

Jason and Rita sat down on the warm sand, and looked at each other without saying a word. A coast guard boat arrived; on it there were newspaper and television reporters. They took all sorts of pictures of the Inspector posing with the statue. Two police officers escorted Jason and Rita to the yacht to pick up their belongings and their passport.

Jason went and looked for the money that Richard was to pay him, but when he went into Richard's cabin, he saw that the safe was left open. He ran to Cyrus's cabin and searched for the money. Finally, he found the money hidden in Cyrus's closet. He quickly took a count of the money and recounted the money again.

There was almost double the amount what Richard owed him. He grabbed the money and hid the cash in his suitcase.

Rita gathered most of her stuff and some of her father's belongings. When they were finished packing they were escorted off the yacht by the police officer, and taken to the Inspector's police car. Jason and Rita were driven back to their hotel where they were staying.

"These four policemen will stay with you until you are ready to leave Malta and the sooner the better," the Inspector warned them before he drove away.

The day after, the Inspector visited Jason and Rita at the hotel. He entered their room and handed Jason a copy of the newspaper.

"You are a very popular man today," said Jason. "And they are going to give you a promotion also? Maybe I should tell them who found the statue."

"Yes, you do that and maybe I will tell them how the small boat blew up, and perhaps you go to jail," said the Inspector pulling a piece of rope from his pocket. "Too bad you have to leave today. Tomorrow we are going to have a feast to celebrate the finding."

"We haven't any choice now, do we?" answered Jason.

"Yes, you can stay, only if you promise me that you won't get into any more trouble," replied the Inspector.

"You mean we can stay?" joyfully asked Rita.

"Yes. Only two days. I made all the arrangements for you two," the Inspector informed them.

The day after, there was a big celebration in Malta.

The Inspector received his promotion to captain. Jason and Rita spent the last days in Malta visiting the historic site. Rita was moved as she entered the St. Paul's catacombs in Rabat, and the temples of Hagar Qim. She had received the best history lesson that she ever had in her life. The two days went by. A police car picked up Jason and Rita from the hotel and drove them to the airport as the new police captain was waiting for them.

"Well, the most popular man in Malta. What nobility for you to see us leaving Malta," Jason said with a smile.

"Thanks to you, I've become a captain and found the treasure," said the Inspector.

"Well, we found it and you took the credit," said Jason.

"Yes, that is true, but it's better for you this way. You could have stayed in jail for a long time," said the Inspector smiling.

"Captain, what is your name, anyway?" Jason asked with curiosity.

"Eduardo, in English is Dwight," replied the Inspector. "Captain Dwight. That is my name."

A police officer informed the new police captain that the plane was waiting for Jason and Rita to board. The Inspector walked with Jason and Rita to the plane entrance and before Jason boarded the plan he told the police captain, "Captain, you better guard that golden Falcon very good. One of these days, I will come back and steal it from under your nose. I promise. That's mine," smiled Jason.

"You do that, and you will never leave Malta again. I hope not, my friend. If you do decide to steal it, please wait until I retire," said Captain Dwight.

Jason and Rita walked up the steps to the plane. "You didn't mean that, did you?" Rita asked Jason.

"Oh, yes I did," replied Jason. They waved at the Captain and went inside the plane.

The plane lifted off and was on its way to the United States of America.

Captain Dwight took a deep breath. "I want double the security around the Maltese Falcon, twenty-four hours a day," ordered the Captain.

"What for?" asked the sergeant.

"I have a feeling that he will be coming back. He always keeps his promise," said the Captain as he headed to his car and drove away. "Now I am going on vacation."

The End

In memory of my parents. Maryann and Charlie Fenech. Gone but Never Forgoten.

Mario Fenech

CPSIA information can be obtained at www.ICGtesting.com
Printed in the USA
LVOW132351220113

316800LV00001B/17/P